Copyright © 2022 Briony Marshall

Published by TWH Publishing
www.thewritinghall.co.uk

All rights reserved. The author asserts their moral right under the Copyright, Designs and Patents Act 1988 to be identified as the author of this work.

Cover design by Stephen Caile

Except for the quotation of small passages for the purposes of criticism and review, no part of this publication may be reproduced, stored in a retrieval system, or transmitted, in any form or by any means, electronic, mechanical, photocopying, recording or otherwise, without the prior consent of the publisher at the address above.

ISBN 978-1-9998669-8-3

From Rags to Richie

by
Briony Marshall

For all my fellow day dreamers, keep it up! Dreams really do come true.

Chapter One

'We're a very expensive group; we break a lot of rules. It's unheard of to combine opera with a rock theme, my dear.' ~ Freddie Mercury

'I think it's disgusting, charging so much for something with so little material.' The lines on Mrs Delong's face contorted as she spoke. 'I bet they can knock out five of these from a metre!'

I tried not to sigh. My customer service skills, as a rule, came easily enough, but when it came to Mrs Delong, *nothing* was easy.

'Pinching...that's what it's all about these days. Pinching!' She put on an exaggerated voice. 'Oh, I'll just pinch an inch from here then pinch a pound more from the customer's pocket. No one will notice. Well, news flash, everyone, it's obvious what you're all doing when clothes cost a fortune and they just don't fit.' She lifted the corner of a dress and added, 'The only thing that's good for is a twig!'

Mrs Delong was the unofficial winner of Belle's Boutique's 'Ultimate Customer Complaint Award' three years in a row. She was a handful at the best of times, but especially when you were working a shift on your own.

'It's a size small, Mrs Delong. The label states that just here. I thought we agreed last month that a medium suited you better?' I could feel my smile cracking.

'But I got a size small last week!'

'That was a batwing jumper, Mrs Delong. They have a little more...give.' I inwardly winced as I said this. Size was such a delicate issue in the fashion industry.

'Fine,' Mrs Delong tutted. 'If you could just arrange my refund, dearie, I'll be on my way.'

I opened the till drawer and handed her forty

pounds. Then I lifted a pair of seamstress scissors from underneath the counter and snipped away one of the beautiful, faceted buttons from the front of the dress.

Mrs Delong gasped and clutched the string of pearls at her neck. 'Why did you do that?'

'As a regular customer, Mrs Delong, I'm sure you're aware of our company policy. I'm only allowed to give refunds on faulty items.' *At least now, my aunt won't kill me when she finds out I've given you your money back yet again.*

'This is absurd! This place, it's gone mad.' With that, she flounced through the door.

'See you next week, Mrs Delong,' I called as the bell above the door chimed.

'Trouble in paradise, Penny?' I looked up to see a familiar face grinning at me.

'Dad!'

'Is your aunt about?' His eyes darted from left to right in mock fear.

'No, luckily. Though you have just missed Mrs Delong.'

'The serial bringer-backerer?'

I chuckled. He did listen to me. 'The very same.'

'I was hoping to steal you away a little early,' he said. 'We could grab a coffee. I've got something exciting to tell you.'

I looked at the clock. 4pm. Still half an hour to go. 'Aw, Dad, these last thirty minutes are going to be torture now.'

'Promise it'll be worth it. Meet you at The Stag in thirty-five?'

'That escalated quickly...from coffee to a pint? Stay classy, Dad. I'll see you in a bit.'

***

As I entered The Stag, I spotted Dad immediately. His grin lit up the whole pub. As I reached his table, I was pleased to see a cappuccino already waiting for me.

'Thanks, Dad.' I kissed him on the cheek before settling

in the seat opposite. 'So, to what do I owe the pleasure?'

Ever since my parents spilt seven years ago, Dad's visits always came with a fanfare. That he'd met me from work was a first.

'Like I said, I've got something exciting to tell you. Ready?'

I didn't know what to expect; my dad was a dreamer. In fact, I was convinced that this was what had torn my parents apart. There comes a time in everyone's life when they need to grow up and I think Dad never got that memo—despite being married and having a house and kid.

'I think I've finally found it...your big break! Get you out of Belle's Boutique once and for all.'

I frowned. 'Aunt Ange has put her life and soul into that business, don't be so facetious.'

He dismissed my protests with a wave of his hand. 'I'm serious, Pen, hear me out. Do you remember Rodger? The guy I use to riff with back in the day? 'Rodger the Dodger'?'

All aboard Dad's train of daydreams. 'Uh-huh...'

'Well, he got in touch last night, because he'd heard some news and remembered you. Wasn't that nice of him?'

My fake customer service smile made a reappearance.

'Rodge's brother, he's also into the music biz...though not in the same way as me and Rodge, more composing and mixing different sounds together, stuff like that. He's done alright for himself, you know, composed a couple of soundtracks for a few TV shows. Nothing major, but still, something to talk about.' He paused for my reaction.

I took a sip of my coffee. It wasn't that I was uninterested, I was just all too aware of Dad's tall stories and hair-brained schemes.

'Anyway, he was on the phone to Rodge the other night. He's been hired by this company that's making some fancy period drama show for the telly next year.

And, in casual conversation, like, he mentioned they were looking for people. Not for the music...me and Rodge wouldn't be much good with something like that.' He chuckled to himself before taking a sip of his beer.

'No...' he wiped his lips with the back of his hand, 'not really our scene and all that. They need help with the costumes and wardrobe and stuff. Instantly, Rodge thought of you and your fashion degree. As soon as he put the phone down, he called me. He's sent me the website and everything to apply. Pen, it looks dead good. If nothing else, it's a step in the right direction. Let me show you...' He reached for his phone, but I'd already grabbed my bag.

'I'd better go, Dad. Mum will be wondering where I've got to.'

'But, Penny, I haven't even shown you the details yet.'

'Don't worry about it. I won't be applying.'

He looked wounded. 'Why the hell not? It's not like it's far away. They're filming on the moors, making use of all the scenery and Shuderly Castle.'

'Honestly, it's okay. Tell Rodger I'm very grateful that he thought of me.' I turned to leave.

'You don't understand. I honestly think this could be your chance!'

I stopped in my tracks, before whirling round. 'Chance at what, Dad? I haven't even looked at my design work since the day I graduated. My sketchbooks are at home, collecting dust. They'll want someone out there who's already working in the field, not someone working part-time in her aunt's clothes shop. I'm not being unappreciative; I'm just being realistic. It's really sweet that you believe in me so passionately, but it's a little too late for me, I'm afraid.' I stared at my shoes. I felt like I was about to cry.

'How will you know if you don't take the chance?'

'What? And upset Mum, Aunt Ange and potentially lose my job? Just for someone to say, 'Sorry, thanks, but no'? I'll stick with the boutique.'

'That's called playing it safe. You know how I feel about playing it safe, Pen.' He looked stern. Clearly, this was not how he'd believed the conversation would go.

'That's exactly my point. This is me, not you.'

'Promise me you'll at least think about it. Take a look at the application, I'm emailing it now.'

I gave him a wave as I slipped out of the pub doors.

Chapter Two

At home, within the familiar four walls of my bedroom, comforted by the songs of Queen, I concluded that I was the perfect blend of my parents' personalities. I'd managed to cool down enough from my conversation with Dad to explain everything to Mum and, over dinner, I'd both agreed and disagreed with the things she had to say on the issue. Niggling me now were my own desires.

I definitely had a creative side, a passion. It didn't manifest in the same way as Dad's, through music, but I had completed a degree in the field of fashion and design. Back then, I'd had a flair for how one adorned their body, with my nineties' highlights and swish, modern 'lob'. I still had the edginess of a girl who lived with her finger on the pulse of fashion, even though I'd graduated more than five years ago. Now, though, I had another side, a part that appreciated stability and being able to pay my bills, one that celebrated achieving the little things—like making a house feel like a home.

I decided I was a realist with a dream, someone who also had the ability to prioritise. Right now, saving as much money as I could afford to would allow me to move out of my mum's house in the not-so-distant future. That was way more important than risking everything, just so that a small-scale period drama team would accept me into their wardrobe department, temporarily.

Happy with my conclusion, *Queen*, as if on cue, told me otherwise.

'I want it all, and I want it now.'

I rolled over and reached for my phone. *It wouldn't hurt to look, right? It's not a commitment. It's not like if I just look at the application I've applied.* It was the least

I could do, and I wouldn't come across as a spoilt brat to Dad. I'd be able explain why it wasn't for me, that it would no doubt ask for experience and skills I didn't have.

Taking a deep breath, I opened Dad's email.

My eyes flitted across the screen. The job title was for a 'Wardrobe Assistant'. Maybe it wasn't as out of my league as I thought.

The application asked for a standard C.V., job history, and experience relevant to the field. Design sketches were not a necessity, though they could be included if desired. *Not exactly rocket science.*

Maybe I have enough to put together an application... My university portfolio could work, my C.V. was up to date, and I'd helped with enough fashion shows and photoshoots to generate publicity for the boutique over recent years.

I locked my phone. Maybe a few years ago, this could have been a turning point. But they say comfort is the enemy of progress, and I couldn't think of any truer words in that moment. Everything had worked out: I had a job, a car, somewhere to live. Okay, maybe a boyfriend would have made my life a little more complete, but after my last relationship had crashed and burned at the end of university, and I'd also had a front row seat for my parents' breakup, love didn't seem the be all and end all for me anymore. Why fix something that wasn't broken? My happiness was my main priority, and if that meant sticking where I was for the long haul and celebrating small successes, that was exactly what I was going to do.

***

Arriving at Belle's Boutique the next morning, I was surprised but happy to see Aunt Ange already inside. Instead of her usual warm greeting, I was met with a steely-eyed look. Something wasn't right.

'Your mum called last night. I think you and I need to talk.'

Uh-oh. Obediently, I took a seat beside her. I wrapped my hands around the mug waiting for me. As flippantly as possible, I asked, 'What did she call you about?'

'This wardrobe job.'

'Oh.' I shifted in my seat. 'That. I was going to tell you about that...eventually. Mum probably got the wrong end of the stick. It's just Dad and his big ideas, you know what he's like. Nothing to worry about, he'll have forgotten about it this time next week.'

Aunt Ange raised her perfectly defined brows. 'Really, Penny. Take this as advice from a woman who missed almost every opportunity in her life. Don't dismiss this so easily.'

I felt a pang of guilt in my stomach. Aunt Ange had always been my role model. To me, she was the epitome of glamour and fashion. As a child, I'd shuffled round the living room in her kitten heels, smeared her lipstick on my face and emptied her perfume on myself to 'smell pretty'. Aunt Ange's dream was always to walk the catwalk, but a stiletto-based ankle injury in her teens had put an abrupt end to that. Her love for fashion didn't die, though; it instead led her to opening Belle's Boutique. That said, I knew that it had never fully satisfied her ambition.

'Aunt Ange, don't be silly. I can't just leave you, the business and my life to chase some pipe dream.'

'Sure, you can. What have you got to lose?'

'Everything!'

Aunt Ange laughed. 'Your life has only just begun, sweetheart. Trust me. This is exactly the right time to shake things up a little.'

'But...' I started.

'Penny, stop putting barriers in the way. I hate to admit it but, for once, your father's right. You've got to grab this opportunity with both hands. Now go home and get your application in before it's too late.' I opened my mouth again and she raised her hand to silence me. 'I mean it, I don't want to see you until it's done.'

***

My fingers hovered over the keyboard, my C.V. on the screen. After a thorough read through, it appeared that I fit the job description perfectly. My experience in the field, though on a small scale, was ample. The only unknowns were my sketches. My style was a little offbeat. I liked to take elements from various trends and turn them on their head a little...match blue with green, for example. Adding an exaggerated bow to a formal suit. Accessorising a monochrome look with vivid pops of colour. None of it screamed 'period drama'.

I heard the front door opening.

'Penny, are you home?' Mum shouted up the stairs.

'Yeah.' I closed my laptop and headed downstairs.

'I thought you were working today, honey?'

'Aunt Ange sent me home.'

'Oh, why? Is everything okay? Are you sick?' Instinctively, Mum touched my forehead.

I laughed and batted her hand away. 'A little birdie told her about a certain job application I was avoiding. And now I'm not allowed to return to work until it's been sent in. Any ideas who that could have been?'

'Well, erm...how's it going?'

'Fine.' I felt my shoulders droop a little. 'Well, it *was* going fine. I want to send some costume sketches in with my application, but I haven't got any and I don't have time to start from scratch.'

'I've got an hour before I'm back in the office. Want me to take a look?'

Within minutes, the kitchen became overrun with pages from my sketchbooks; every surface, counter, and even the cooker, became littered with paper. Mum sat on the floor; pages spread out before her. I sat at the kitchen table, scrutinising drawings I hadn't looked at in years.

'What about this one?' Mum passed me one of the pages from her stack.

It bore the silhouette of a tall, slim lady who sported

a white A-line gown with a lace corset top and pearl beading. 'Oh, that! It's from the bridal collection I designed in my second year.'

'Yeah, but that's only because you're looking at it like that,' she said. 'Maybe if you lengthened the bodice into a V-shape, changed the colour scheme a little and puffed out the skirt... It's definitely giving me 'Marie Antoinette' vibes.'

'I suppose.' I tilted my head, trying to see her vision.

Mum looked at her watch. 'Is that the time?! Honey, I've got to go. Dan will be wondering where the hell I've got to. You've got this, trust me. A few alterations on your bridal sketches and you're good to go. When's the deadline again?'

'Tomorrow. 10am.'

'No time like the present. I'll see you later.' She gathered up her bag and phone, kissed me on the forehead and headed out the door.

I clutched my bridal portfolio, my mind swimming with ideas. *Indeed. No time like the present.* I opened my case of art supplies and set to work.

Chapter Three

Dear Miss James,

We are delighted to invite you to attend an interview for the role of WARDROBE ASSISTANT with FBW Productions...

I must have read the start of that email around fifty times within the first few minutes of receipt. Excitement made my heart thump hard in my chest. Any fears I had about stagnation evaporated. I picked up my phone to tell Mum the news just as the bell above the boutique door rang. *Keep calm, Pen, you've got this. Just serve this customer then you can scream down the phone and dance around to your heart's content... Maybe close for lunch first, though.*

I looked up to see Dad in the doorway.

'You're not going to believe what I've got to show you!' I quickly flipped the shop sign to 'closed' and loaded up the email, presenting it to Dad with a grin to rival the Cheshire Cat's.

His eyes flitted across the screen as he read the message. 'That's fantastic news!' He scooped me up into an embrace.

'Thanks, Dad.' I squeezed him tightly before letting go. 'I think I owe you an apology.'

'Don't worry about it, kiddo. I knew you'd come to your senses eventually. It's scary, taking risks, putting yourself out there. Trust me, I know. But, sometimes, you've just got to go for it.'

'Aunt Ange gave me a good talking to. She was the one who pushed me to do it in the end. She wouldn't let me come back to work until I'd applied!'

'Wait, hold on a minute. Are you telling me that your Aunt Ange sided with me?!' Dad clutched his chest in mock shock. 'Shoot me down, I never thought I'd see the day when we agreed on anything!'

I shoved him playfully. 'You make it sound like you hate each other.'

'I thought we did!' However, the sly smile and glint in his eye said otherwise.

***

I couldn't remember the last time I'd attended a job interview—or any interview, for that matter. Working for my aunt had been more of a rite of passage than anything else, and my university interview had been nothing more than a casual chat. I'd walked into the room sporting my 'Lavish Alice' cape blazer and the tutor couldn't take her eyes off it. The rest was history.

I took a deep breath. I felt like a fish out of water in the minimalist waiting room.

'Penelope James?'

'Oh, yes, here.' I jumped up and headed towards the person peeking through the open door. 'Call me Penny.' I shook the lady's hand. Her fingers were long and beautifully manicured, her hands as cold as ice.

'Sure. Hello, Penny, please come in. Take a seat.' She gestured to an executive chair that sat opposite a large desk. Behind the desk were three more chairs, two of which were occupied by two men who looked to be in their mid-to-late forties.

I gave them my best smile. 'Good afternoon.'

***

Back home—Mum and Aunt Ange all ears—I recounted the experience.

'So, you met the Production Manager of FBW Productions and told him all about Belle's Boutique?' Aunt Ange fanned herself.

I laughed. I was quite sure that she didn't have a clue who the Production Manager of FBW Productions even was, let alone cared whether he knew about her business or not. But then she'd always been a fan of celebrity culture, no matter how small or obscure.

'So, what happened after you'd all finished talking?'

From Rags to Richie

Mum was literally on the edge of her seat.

'They sent me back to the waiting room, and when I got there, two girls and a guy had appeared. We all sat awkwardly looking at each other for twenty minutes then they started calling us in, one by one.'

I sipped my coffee. It was fun, keeping my audience on tenterhooks.

'They called the guy in first. He wasn't in the room long, though. When they'd finished he just left.'

'Ooh, did he look upset?' said Aunt Ange.

'A little, it was hard to tell. He was gone in a flash.'

'Oh dear, that can't have been good news then,' said Mum.

'Then they started on us girls,' I continued. 'The youngest went first. She must have only been out of uni a year. She was with them a little longer than the guy. And when she left, she was thanking them all profusely for the opportunity. Then it was the turn of the girl who looked to be a similar age to me. She was covered in designer labels.'

Aunt Ange tutted and received a nudge from her sister. 'What? It just annoys me when people think they can buy their way into people's good books. Labels are beautiful, but money isn't everything.'

'Back in the day, you walked around in your fair share of designer brands. Come on, Ange!'

'Well, you know what I mean. I admit, I loved designer gear in my time, but not all at once, and definitely not with the sole purpose of clinching a job interview.' The two women exchanged a knowing look before dissolving into laughter.

Mum composed herself. 'Sorry, honey, we digress.'

'Aside from the labels, she was really nice,' I said. 'She complimented my outfit when we were the only two in the waiting room, and when she left, she gave me a lovely smile.'

'So, I guess it was your turn then?'

'Uh-huh.' I could tell the suspense was killing them

and it was so entertaining to watch. Mum's fingers tapped the side of her coffee cup and Aunt Ange began chewing her lip.

'Well...' I slowly placed my mug on the table, 'when I got back into the room, they were all smiles. It turned out that the four of us were the entire shortlist, the cream of the crop. They said there was something about my application they really liked. In fact, Win, she's the head of Wardrobe, complimented my sketches. She thought they were, and I quote, 'utterly unique'.'

I couldn't keep them in suspense any longer. 'So, I'm sorry to do this to you, Aunt Ange, especially at such short notice, but I'm afraid I won't be able to make my shift on Monday...because I got the job!'

The sisters squealed and jumped up from their seats to smother me in kisses. I wished I could have taken a picture and captured that very moment forever.

'Well done, darling,' Aunt Ange whispered in my ear. 'I knew you'd do it.'

Chapter Four

'Good morning, Penny. So glad to have you with us.' As promised, at ten o'clock the following Monday, Win was awaiting my arrival in the office foyer, holding a lanyard, a clipboard, and a set of keys. She handed me all three. 'Welcome to FBW Productions.'

'Thank you.'

'You're welcome.' Win's smile was perfect. 'Now, let's get your photo done for your pass then I'll introduce you to everyone in our office.' She headed towards the lifts.

The building reminded me of my university days. It was welcoming, but in a clinical way. The corridors seemed to go on for days, weaving in and out and around each other. I felt it would be easy to get lost.

We made a brief stop along one corridor, where a nice, smiley guy called Stan took my photo and within minutes handed Win the result. She asked me for the lanyard she'd handed over just minutes earlier and slid the FBW branded key-card into the plastic holder on the end. She then placed the lanyard around my neck delicately and precisely, as if she were awarding me a knighthood. 'Welcome to the family.' She smiled before turning on her heel and ushering us through even more corridors.

We came to a halt outside a large door. 'Wardrobe' was emblazoned across its front in the same way a star's name would be written on their dressing room door.

'And this is us.' Win reached for her key card then thought better of it. 'Try yours,' she gestured.

It felt like a 'pinch me' moment as I lifted the little white card up to the scanner. The black box gave a merry bleep and the lock on the door clicked as it released.

'Perfect!' Win beamed. 'Come on in.'

The room was empty of people, which meant the first thing I noticed were the desks; all four of them were littered with paperwork, pencils, paints, laptops, sewing machines and glue guns. Clothing rails were against every wall, some bowing under the weight of many garments. Others were completely bare, with notes taped to their poles, hinting at their future content. Win led us to a desk at the far end of the room. It was the largest of the four.

'This is us. Let's get you a seat.' Win was a petite lady, and it was painful to watch her haul a chair from the corner of the room. She refused my help and eventually settled it next to hers. She took a seat and beckoned me to do the same.

She picked up a fancy mechanical pencil and started jotting on a Post-it note. 'Everyone's on a coffee break at the moment, they'll soon be back.' She lowered her voice to a whisper, 'Technically, you're here to assist the whole department, but I was the only one on the interview panel. Stick with me, honey, and you'll go places.'

I was still deciding how to respond when the beep of the door sounded, and the rest of team filed in. Each of them gave me a warm smile or a small wave before they sat down.

Once they were settled, Win moved to the front of the room and signalled for me to join her. 'Right then, girls, time for me to introduce our newest recruit. This is Penny, our new Wardrobe Assistant. I hope you've practised your introductory speeches.' She let out a shrill laugh, but no one joined in with her. 'I'm only joking, ladies, don't look so concerned!'

'That's Deb, she's our best seamstress.' Win gestured to the woman sitting at the desk next to ours at the back of the room. Deb was a short brunette with bright blue eyes and rosy cheeks. She had a friendly face and gave off a motherly vibe. 'Absolute whizz with a sewing machine, she is. She sorts all our last-minute alterations and repairs.' I saw Deb blush, even though her cheeks were already ruddy.

'I try my best, said Deb, batting away the compliment. 'By the time you reach my age, dear, you've had plenty of practice.' She smiled at me, her whole face lighting up as she did so.

'I don't know, I'm not sure I can improve my speed that much in what...three years?' I replied.

'Ooh...you can stay!' Deb cooed.

'And this is Suzie,' prompted Win. 'She's our concept artist.'

Suzie looked up from the sketch she was working on. 'Hey,' she said warmly. With her pastel pink pixie cut and odd earrings, I recognised a kindred spirit. She was of a similar age to me, and an edginess radiated from her. Though we'd only been in the same room for less than five minutes I knew we'd get along just fine.

'She sees to the creation sketches and sourcing materials,' Win continued. 'But she's always on hand if anything needs reviewing and such.' Win craned her neck to squint at Suzie's drawing. Suzie opened her mouth to say something, but Win had already moved on.

'And this is Bella. She's Wardrobe Maintenance. She ensures that, once all the costumes are within our possession, they're kept safe, clean and in order.'

'I'm a dream with steam,' Bella added, pressing the button on the machine she held. A small steam cloud escaped that made everyone laugh. Bella was tall and slender with long, sleek blonde hair. She turned back to the gown she'd been steaming.

Win sat back at 'our' desk. 'We all have a hand in sewing, creation and upkeep, but we each focus on a key area, if you will.' She paused for dramatic effect. 'And then there's me, the visionary! I'm here to bring the costumes to life...the bridge between our office and the spotlight. I meet the actors and deal with their requests.

I help to dress them on set and ensure continuity for the camera. I give skirts a fluffing when the need arises and untuck shirts when they need to be untucked.'
She winked suggestively. For the second time that day I contemplated how to react. I gave an innocent smile. Not disagreeing, but not completely agreeing either. *Win/Win. No pun intended.*

'Your role as assistant is to help the team in any way you can. Using your full skillset to add a fresh new voice from design all the way to dress. I hope you're ready, Penny.' I nodded enthusiastically.

'Fabulous. You'll have time to get to know the girls better later, as I've got an important meeting to attend soon. For now, though...' she lifted a large pile of documents onto the desk, 'could you go through these papers? They're rental receipts from companies we're hoping to hire from. Could you give each one a call to confirm they've received our deposit and that all the information we have is the same as theirs? Oh, and please double-check their dates for delivery, so that everything is here and ready for next week.'

I quickly leafed through the pile. That didn't seem too bad. 'Sure,' I said, smiling back at her.

'Fantastic. Thank you.' Win grabbed her bag and headed for the door. 'So, yes, Penny, these are the girls. Girls, this is Penny. See you all later!' Just as she was about to leave, she turned to add, 'You need to press four before making any external calls.' She pointed to the Post-it note she'd written on earlier. 'I've left my number but do only use it if there's an emergency. Ciao, ladies!' Then she was gone.

The atmosphere in the office changed instantly. It was as if a weight had been lifted and the mute button removed. The women gathered around my desk, chatting animatedly.

'Aw, it's so nice to have a new face in the office,' Suzie said, beaming. 'Us creatives work better in numbers.' There was a chorus of agreement.

'Do you need any help with that?' Deb nodded towards the documents Win had left me.

'Oh, no...but thank you. I think I can handle it.' A look of disapproval crossed Deb's face as she eyed the pile of papers. 'I'd better get cracking. Thanks for the warm welcome. I still can't believe I'm here, to be honest.'

'Bless you. Well, if you need any help, you know where we are.' Bella returned to her steamer.

I smiled. 'I thought 'assisting' was my job.' They grinned back at me. 'Thanks, though, it means a lot.'

It took the rest of the day to work through Win's documents. She never returned from her meeting, so I just took my breaks and left for home at the same time as the others. Overall, I felt that my first day had been a success.

To celebrate, Mum had invited Aunt Ange and Dad to have dinner with us. It was the first time all of us had sat at the same table in three years. She was making her signature spaghetti Bolognese, my absolute favourite.

I walked in the door and there they all were, expectant smiles on their faces.

'So, how did it go?' asked Mum.

'Great, actually. Really good. I have my own ID card and everything.' I waved my lanyard around like it was a prize. Mum clapped her hands together.

Dad nudged my arm as Mum served up the food. 'Sounds like it's all coming together then, Pen.' I couldn't stop the grin spreading across my face.

It felt like we were a family once again. And it seemed like my life was finally going somewhere. *What could tomorrow bring to top this?*

Chapter Five

'So, you commute, am I right?' I'd run into Win in the Starbucks' queue the next morning, so we walked to the office together.

'Uh-huh,' I replied, mid-sip. *This caramel macchiato is so good.*

'Could you get here earlier if need be?'

Here we go, the overtime chat. To be honest, my commute wasn't horrendous, though it would be quicker if I'd only brave the motorway. 'Definitely,' I said. First impressions were still being formed.

'Fabulous! In that meeting yesterday, Carl mentioned he'd arranged minibuses to get all the crew and equipment to where we're filming on day one. I wanted to reserve you a place. I'm going to need my assistant on set from the get go.'

Excitement fizzed within me. 'Oh, Win, I'd love that!'

'I thought you would. It'll be fun. Carl was all for it when I told him how well you took to everything yesterday. Like I said, stick with me, honey, and you'll go places. The interviews were all about trying to find someone to enhance our team, and I definitely think we've found her!' By now, we'd reached the lifts to our office. Win stopped me getting in and lowered her voice. 'The other girls don't know about this; it's probably best we don't mention anything until Carl does. Don't want to make things awkward, now, do we? Right, I've just got to nip somewhere before we start work. See you up there.'

'Sure.' I smiled.

Win headed in the opposite direction. I couldn't quite figure her out just yet, but if she was offering opportunities like that on day two, I didn't want to get on the wrong side of her.

It was after the morning coffee break when Win arrived in the office. She looked drained; she'd lost all the colour from her cheeks and her hair stuck out at random angles. The others just stared at her before carrying on with their work.

Win didn't seem to care. She made a beeline for me. 'My black and gold notebook, have you seen it?' Her eyes looked glazed, as if she wasn't fully in the moment.

'Er, I'll have a look for it. Is it on the desk?'

'It should be in my handbag,' she muttered, 'but it's not there.'

After a bit of searching, I found it under a pile of papers. 'Is this it?'

'Oh my god, Penny, you're a lifesaver!' Win clutched the book to her chest. 'I owe you one,' she shouted as she raced out of the room.

I smiled as she retreated down the corridor. Although Win seemed a high-powered businesswoman, she had her blonde moments. The other girls seemed uninterested in Win's dilemma—I even noticed Bella rolling her eyes as Win left.

I had a niggling feeling, a hint that there was something going on I wasn't privy to. I opened my mouth to say something, to question the suddenly silent room, but I closed it again. It was only my second day; I couldn't get sucked into any office drama so early in the job.

'Did anyone catch that new quiz show last night?' Suzie asked, a pin between her teeth.

The consensus was no, so Suzie launched into a detailed explanation of the programme. I sat next to Deb and did my best to help her with her sewing project.

Ten minutes before the day ended the phone on Win's desk rang. The girls encouraged me to answer it. 'Hello, Wardrobe. Penny speaking.'

'Penny!' came Win's voice. 'Just the person. Do you have to scoot off straightaway?'

I didn't have a commitment on Tuesday nights...or

any night, for that matter. 'Er, no, I don't have anything planned tonight. Why, what's up?'

'I've got a small job I'd like your help with if that's okay?'

'Sure. Where do you need me, shall I come now?'

'Oh, you're such a sweetie. Meet me outside the canteen in ten minutes.'

'Okay.' My stomach fluttered. I didn't even know what the job was, yet I was already excited.

'See you in a sec,' said Win. 'Bye.'

Putting the receiver back, I felt an urge to seek the girls' opinions about what Win might need me to do. But they already had their coats on. I thought back to what Win had said that morning and felt that the less said, the better—for now.

'Penny, you coming?' Bella held the door open.

'Erm, thanks, but something's come up.' I nodded towards the phone. 'I'll see you tomorrow.'

She smiled. 'Make sure Win doesn't work you too hard, now. See you in the morning.'

I tidied our desk and tucked in the chairs to give the girls time to vacate the building before I went to the canteen. When I got there, the lights were off, and all the chairs were upside down on the tables. Unsure what to do, I hovered at the door, hoping to spot Win.

She emerged from a door on the other side of the corridor. 'So glad you could make it. You're in for a treat!' She linked her arm through mine and walked me through the corridor at a pace. We stopped suddenly outside another door. Win straightened her skirt, smoothed down my hair and took a deep breath.

'Ready?'

I nodded, but I couldn't shift the uneasy feeling I had deep down. She opened the door and led me into the biggest office I'd ever seen. Stretching across the wall space was an array of certificates and photographs of people in fancy suits and gowns. The walls themselves were dove grey with walnut panelling—the chairs, table and filing cabinet matched the scheme. At the table, two men sat opposite one another. One poured whiskey from a decanter. They were laughing about something that had been said before we'd entered.

Win cleared her throat and approached the table. She gestured to one of the men. 'Penny, this is Carl Wright, the Executive Producer. I don't think you've met.'
Finally, the infamous Carl Wright. The gentleman had a kind but stern face. There were lines around his mouth and his eyes were deep set. He owned the space he was in; even without speaking, you could tell he was not the kind of person you'd cross.

He extended his hand and gave me a pearly white smile. 'Hello, Penny, lovely to meet you. Welcome to FBW Productions.' I took his hand. His grip was firm, the practiced handshake of an accomplished businessman.

'Thank you.' I returned his handshake with as much vigour as I could muster. I was trying to think of the right words to compliment his Hugo Boss suit, but Win chimed in with a second introduction before I could speak.

'And this is Richie Clarke...*our star!*' She emphasised the last part, which Richie shrugged off with a laugh. He got to his feet to shake my hand.
Wow! First Carl Wright, now Richie Clarke. RICHIE CLARKE! I couldn't believe it. I shook Richie's hand. Stay cool, Pen, stay cool.

My knowledge of popular culture outside the fashion world was limited. I was still into *Queen*, for heaven's sake. Yet I knew this guy's name. Richie Clarke could be the dictionary's definition for 'tall, dark and handsome'. He'd been a household name for a few years, his genre being love stories. If there was a show that needed a heartthrob or a criminal mastermind that could make you swoon, Richie was your man.

Richie was in his early forties. His wall calendar was the type of thing you'd buy your Mum for Christmas, though it would double as a secret gift for you, so you could stare at his likeness all year round. He was a favourite in 'Most Gorgeous Man Alive' polls and he had plenty of trophies from TV award ceremonies.

His sexy persona was predominantly for the camera, however—various news outlets had confirmed that he was happily married with baby number two on the way.

'Hey.' His voice was as smooth and velvety as dark chocolate.

'Hi.' I exhaled the word. Richie just smiled and waited for me to take the seat being offered by Carl before he returned to his own.

'Penny will be assisting Win on set with wardrobe and such,' said Carl. 'I thought it best we all get acquainted now while we have chance.' Win had taken a seat next to him and was now pouring herself some wine. She filled a glass of the same for me.

Richie took the opportunity to take a long look at me. His smile lingered.

'To new beginnings.' Carl raised his glass. 'Happy to finally have you on board, Richie.'

'Cheers.' Richie tilted his glass to his lips and took a long, slow swig of whiskey. The motion emphasised his strong jawline. He really was a prime example of classic good looks.

'Cheers.' Win echoed. I responded by raising my glass. Of all the ways I thought my second day could end, not once did I think I'd be spending it with Richie Clarke.

Chapter Six

The next morning, I felt like I was about to explode. *Last night I shared a drink with Richie Clarke!* I desperately wanted to tell the other women in the department, but I had a feeling that would be a bad move. I hated the apparent divide. I wanted to stay neutral—I was assistant to the whole department, after all, but Win was persuasive. Ultimately, she was offering me some incredible opportunities.

In the last couple of days there hadn't been one mention of the name 'Richie Clarke' on the project, yet I'd been helping to create the clothes that would encompass his body. I forced myself to stop visualising Richie getting in and out of said clothes. *Oh my god, is that something I'll have to bear witness to at some point?!* All I'd known about the current project was this…it was the tale of a forbidden romance during the French Revolution. The costumes were all puffy skirts and blue tailcoats. Alongside the male and female leads would be a whole host of supporting cast members and extras.

The main location was Shuderly Castle and its surrounding moorland. Further interior locations were yet to be confirmed. The production was called *Love and War*—or at least that's what I'd seen written everywhere.

There didn't seem to be anything for me to do, other than shadow one of the other women yet again. In a ballsy move that was unlike me, I called the number Win had left me on my first day. After the third ring, she picked up.

'Win Yung, Wardrobe.'

'Win, it's Penny.' Deb's head flicked up at my words and she met my gaze. After a couple of seconds, she turned back to her work.

'Oh, hi, Penny!' Win's tone changed. 'Is everything

okay?'

Damn, I forgot she told me to only contact her in an emergency. 'Yes, sorry, it's nothing to worry about. I was just wondering if there was anything you needed help with. Everything's under control here, I just wanted to make myself useful.'

'Ooh, Penny, I like you!' Win seemed to appreciate my forwardness. 'I've just got to tie up a few loose ends then you can join me. Another pair of eyes couldn't hurt. Meet me and Craig—that's our director—in the front foyer in a few minutes. We're going on a field trip. Ciao.'

I grabbed my coat. Before I could get to grips with what was happening, I found myself in the back of Craig's car. We drove through country lanes until the lines of hedges broke away and all you could see for miles were vast green and brown hills.

Win sat shotgun, giggling away at Craig's every word. He wasn't what I'd expected, if, indeed, I had any expectations. He wasn't old, but he wasn't young either. His hair was brown with strands of grey shining through, and he was balding on top. His laughter lines were defined and the wrinkles around his eyes didn't iron out when his face relaxed.

After what felt like forever, we pulled into the grounds of Shuderly Castle. As we stepped out of the car, we were greeted by a young woman in a red dress suit. She smiled politely and introduced herself as Kat before shaking our hands, asking our names, and leading us to the front of the property.

Although the main bulk of Shuderly Castle was original, it was largely a ruin. A portion of its interior had been renovated over the last couple of decades, and it now housed a museum dedicated to the castle's history and archives. Accompanying this were function rooms, an exhibition room with built in stage and theatre facilities, and a café/bar—FBW Productions had rented these for the duration.

After signing us in with security at the front desk, Kat

gave us a guided tour of the castle and grounds. I had no idea just how much went on there—from firework displays to drive-in movie nights and murder-mystery dinners. I was rather impressed. At the end of her tour, Kat brought us to the roof of the castle. The view was truly breath-taking. You could see for miles and miles, across an expanse of fields and forests. I regretted that I lived only a fifty-minute drive away, yet I'd never been to Shuderly Castle until now.

I finally tore my eyes away from the stunning view and noticed the others had vanished. Hurriedly, I made my way back down the stone spiral staircase. Towards the bottom, Win and Craig spoke in hushed tones.

'And you're definitely sure he's back on board? Win, without him, the whole project's done for. We wouldn't be able to afford the hire on this place, let alone everything else.'

'I promise you, he's in. I saw him last night with my own eyes and he looked surprisingly well, all things considered. You'd never know he was going through a divorce.'

Not paying attention to my foot placement, I missed the last step and stumbled into view.

'Ah, Penny, there you are!' said Win, seemingly glad of the distraction. 'We're just about to leave.'

***

When we got back to the office it was just after finishing time, so I nipped up to our department for the rest of my things. I expected Win to follow, but as soon as we entered the front foyer, Craig led her to his office. As I reached Wardrobe, the other girls were leaving. Bella, spotting me sprinting down the corridor, held the door open.

'Thanks,' I said breathlessly, quickly slipping inside for my bag and books.

'You've been out most of the day, fancy coming for drink with us?' Bella suggested from the doorway.

I looked over and saw Suzie and Deb behind her.

'Come on,' said Deb. 'It would be nice if you could join us.'

'Just a quick drink and a natter,' added Suzie. 'Nothing fancy.'

It felt nice to be wanted and I figured it would be a good opportunity to show that I wasn't a management suck-up.

'You've twisted my arm. Come on then.'

'Yay! Lead the way, Deb,' said Suzie. 'We can introduce Penny to the local.'

***

'Wait, hold on a minute! Are you telling me we've had Richie Clarke, *the* Richie Clarke, signed to this project all this time?!' It only took a bottle of wine split four ways to loosen my lips. Deb was still taking in the details of my meeting the previous night, and Bella's jaw was almost on the floor.

'So, I've been working to his measurements?' Suzie fanned herself with a napkin.

It was funny watching them display the emotions I'd also struggled to contain.

'I thought he was in the middle of a messy divorce?' Bella chimed in. 'In fact, I'm sure he'd taken a hiatus because of it. His missus only had the baby like a couple of months ago.' We all looked at her. 'What?' she said, a defensive tone to her voice. 'I read the gossip rags on my lunch breaks. Someone as high profile as Richie Clarke, well, he can't expect his dirty laundry not to be plastered all over them.'

'Poor thing,' said Deb. 'It does beg the question, though, if all that is true, why sign up for something like *Love and War*? I know it's *our* pride and joy, but I wouldn't exactly call it a comeback, if you know what I mean.'

We all murmured in agreement.

'You may have a point,' I said, setting down my wine glass. 'Remember Win's mild panic the other day? I believe we almost lost Richie from the line-up. I heard

Win and Craig discussing it earlier today—they must have urged her to talk him round. He certainly seemed on board last night.'

I caught a glimmer of resentment in Deb's eyes. Just I was about to ask her if anything was wrong, Suzie squeezed my arm. 'I've got to ask...is he as drop dead gorgeous in real life?!'

This made me smile. 'There's no camera trickery, the man's a walking oil painting.'

An hour later, we'd finished the bottle of wine and went our separate ways. As I headed to the train station, I felt that the night had seen the beginning of a beautiful friendship. Then I remembered the look on Deb's face when I'd mentioned the meeting in Carl Wright's office. Winning the approval of everyone in Wardrobe may prove more difficult than I'd first thought.

Chapter Seven

My first week at FBW Productions flew by. One week soon turned into two, and before I knew it, I'd been there a month. Tuesday Wardrobe Wine Nights had become a regular occurrence. Despite my best efforts to get Win there, it was always just the four of us.

'I don't think that's a good idea,' Win had said when I asked her along. 'You have fun, though.' She'd turned on her stiletto heels and click-clacked her way down the corridor.

'Maybe she just doesn't like mixing business with pleasure.' Mum said as she chopped vegetables for dinner that evening. 'You could learn from her example.' She shot me a look.

I rolled my eyes. Mum could be so dramatic sometimes.

'Our wine nights are harmless. There's never any witch hunting going on, we just let off some steam. I don't understand why Win feels like she wouldn't be welcome.'

***

The office divide became more apparent as the weeks went by, but it wasn't just Deb who seemed wary of Win. I watched Win pile task after task onto Bella's desk one week, which resulted in a group effort one Friday morning to get the work done on time, as Bella crumbled under the pressure. Win just turned her back on the situation and went to some meeting.

Deb had taken to making sly digs about the things Win did or said, both in her absence and to her face—which, to my surprise, Win accepted without batting an eyelid. I'd even caught Suzie muttering at Win's retreat one afternoon, after a little 'to do' about the exact placement of a frill. I wasn't left unscathed either. A few times, I was the one to whom Win barked commands down the phone or the recipient of a rather curt email. *But didn't that usually happen when people had to work to deadlines?* Win's management style was tough, at best. But, I reasoned, no high-powered businesswoman got anywhere by being everyone's friend. She was harsh at times but, from what I'd seen, she was fair, and she was very good at her job. *Was that enough reason to ostracise someone from the group?*

In the other women's eyes, I was probably teacher's pet, but they'd still taken me under their wing. Their dislike of Win's approach hadn't spilled over onto me. I concluded it could only mean one of two things: one, feelings ran deeper at FBW Productions than an average day at the office, or two, I was being paranoid.

At my seventh Wardrobe Wine Night I decided it was time to get the bottom of it. Filming was nearly upon us. I would be spending even more time with Win. If I were about to walk towards my own execution, the least my new buddies could do was let me know.

'As long as you're completely sure that's the best thing to do,' my mother urged when I told her of my plan. 'Do you trust these ladies enough to tell you the truth? More to the point, do they trust you? If you open the wrong can of worms, the bird may come back to peck your behind.'

'Is that even the proper saying?'

She shrugged. 'Maybe not, but you get my drift.'

'I do, but we message each other on weekends, Mum. I helped Suzie pick out an outfit for her date the other night. I showed Deb how to set up her Etsy store, and Bella has already introduced me to her son. I'm pretty sure I can trust them, and I've given them zero reasons to distrust me.'

Mum gave me a knowing look, but I'd already made my decision. I grabbed my things, ready to leave. 'I know what I'm letting myself in for.'

***

'But, Win, I don't see how we're going to get all the alterations done in time.' Deb got up from her seat and lifted her arms in exasperation.

The office was chaos. All morning, various people had arrived, arms full of costumes. They'd dumped them on any available surface before shoving scrawled notes with measurements under our noses. Absorbed in their video calls, they left briskly while paying no attention to our wide-eyed expressions. Win seemed to have orchestrated the whole thing; she hadn't once stopped to check in and now we were buried under a mountain of period drama attire.

'Deborah, I'm only reiterating your job role,' said Win, completely ignoring the issue as she turned to leave.

'And I'm reiterating that your expectations are unrealistic.'

Win spun round to face her. 'Either it gets done or you're done.'

Deb stood her ground. 'It would be a lot easier if you actually helped.'

'Do I need to remind you who your boss is?' Win hissed.

We all heard her. There was complete silence across the office. For a moment, the pair continued to stare each other down until, slowly, Deb sank back into her seat, the fire of the confrontation still flickering in her eyes.

'Right.' Win addressed the room. 'All of it gets completed today. I don't care how long it takes, or how long you have to stay. Do I need to remind any of you that filming starts tomorrow?'

Win approached our desk. She dropped into the seat next to me but swivelled to face the opposite direction. She popped in her Air Pods and began a business call that consisted of random chitchat and fake laughter. I caught Deb's eye as she glared at the back of Win's head.

'You okay?' I mouthed.

Deb pointed to her computer and a couple of seconds later an email appeared from her. It read: *Nothing I can't handle. I know that can't have been nice for you. I'll explain later. Deb x*

I swiftly deleted the email and gave Deb a quick nod. *Looks like it won't be me opening the can worms after all...*

***

Eventually, we gathered in The Oak, wine in hand. It had been a very long day, but, between the four of us, we'd managed to complete the work. Following her confrontation with Deb, Win never left the office, yet neither did she lift a finger to help. She hadn't uttered another word until the final costume made it to the rail. When she did speak, it was with an icy tone.

'So, can someone please explain to me what the deal is with the Win/Wardrobe divide?' The three women before me exchanged awkward glances.

'She's a bitch,' Deb blurted, 'but you don't need me to tell you that after today's performance.'

'Deb!' scolded the other two. They both looked around warily, as if Win was about to pop out from behind the fruit machine.

Deb shrugged. 'What? The kid needs to know what she's getting herself into.'

There was another pause. Suzie and Bella glared at Deb, most likely for sharing too much. Bella reached for the wine bottle and topped up her glass. Suzie leaned in closer. 'Before you joined us, Penny,' she said, 'there was a shift in the hierarchy.' Her index finger traced the rim of her wine glass.

'Pfft,' Deb scoffed. 'Win leapfrogged me to get the Head of Wardrobe job...she slept her way to the top. There was nothing classy, morally right, or anything surprising about it.'

Silence fell.

'She hasn't the same level of experience as me,' Deb said after a minute or two. 'But she's got the legs. And, apparently, that's what matters around here.'

'Deb!' Suzie chided again. 'I know what happened wasn't fair on you. But can we at least try and remain professional about it?' Deb attempted to butt in, but Suzie talked over her. 'Even if Win didn't display you any courtesy, that's not Penny's fault.'

'Why have you stuck around?' I asked. 'You're an incredible seamstress, surely people in the industry would be begging to take you on?' I didn't understand. If such an incident had revealed everybody's true colours, why stay?

'Penny, you're too kind.' A smile returned to Deb's face. 'Truth be told, I love FBW. It's one of the best gigs I've ever had. It's only since Win started walking around like she owned the place, bossing us all about, like we weren't the ones who took her in and nurtured her stuttering, shy arse.' A raised eyebrow from Bella saw Deb come back into line. 'What I'm trying to say is...she uses everyone, then she goes behind their backs to get what she wants, no matter the consequences.'

'No offence, Penny, but this time three years ago Win was you. The newbie, the assistant, the coffee runner,' Bella added awkwardly whilst Deb took a slug of her wine. I dismissed the unintentional dig with a wave of my hand, indicating for Bella to continue. *At the end of the day, who doesn't start out as a coffee runner?* Even when I'd first joined Aunt Ange, there was no exception. 'Deb was destined to have that job,' Bella went on. 'When Carl first told us he was promoting someone in the department, it just made sense. It would have been perfect. The vacancy was for an experienced seamstress; they'd already written the adverts. We'd seen them. I had a friend of mine in the pipeline, she'd been looking for an opportunity like that for years.'

Deb picked up the story. 'Then we got an email from Carl telling us there'd been a change of plan.' 'For the week prior, there'd been no sign of Win in the office and rumours were flying. Whatever had happened, it wasn't enough to get anyone fired, and Win managed to show Carl that she was capable of all the things Craig and the other 'higher-ups' said she was. So, it was settled.' Deb drank the last of her wine. 'All this being said, Penny, I don't want to put you off. FBW is honestly a great place to be and you're young blood. You could do amazingly well there. I just want to make sure you'll keep your wits about you. Win could very well be your best friend and, if I'm honest, I do think she likes you. But don't be surprised if she stabs you in the back.'

Who was it Win had supposedly slept with? I was dying to know, but on cue Suzie returned from the bar. I hadn't even noticed her get up. 'Anyway, I think that's enough of that for one evening,' said Deb. 'Who's ready for a refill?'

Conversation turned to our normal chitchat about TV shows and our home life until our glasses were drained once more. My mind swirled and I found it difficult to concentrate on what the others were saying.

It was only when Bella called out, 'See you tomorrow!', that my consciousness returned to my body. *Shit!* The following day was the first for filming, meaning I'd be on set. I wasn't likely to see them in the office, but I couldn't tell them that, not after the night's topic.

'See you then,' I replied sheepishly before scampering off. I felt like the worst person in the world. *Had Win already got her claws into me?* Maybe I'd just had a little too much vino on a school night.

Chapter Eight

In my fashion career I'd done many things: succeeded under pressure, kept a cool head in fast paced environments, even done full costume changes in under five minutes. But I'd never worked on something the size of *'Love and War'*. Suddenly, on route to the film set, butterflies began cartwheeling in my stomach.

What if I'm not good enough? What if I can't do it? There were intricate details to nail down in this kind of work, such as continuity. *What if the whole show is a mess because of me!?* My breathing became shallow.

I paused for a second. Was I going to let self-doubt get the better of me? I'd come this far; I couldn't turn back now. I allowed the fresh morning air to still my thoughts as I crossed the office car park, which was full of minibuses, vans, and people hauling equipment about. It worked; I spotted Win and all my troubling thoughts disappeared. She was deep in conversation with a man I'd not met. As I got closer, I noted that she was wearing a little more make up than usual. Her usual slim-fit turtleneck had been replaced by a deep vee. *Oh, Deb, if only you were here to see this...*

'Ah, this is the final part of my tribe.' Win gave me one of her dazzling smiles. I knew her well enough by now to know it was as fake as her eyelashes.

'Morning, Penny, grab your seat. The girls are already on board.'

The girls? I climbed on the minibus Win had gestured towards, not waiting for an introduction to the new guy. Sure enough, the whole of Wardrobe was there. I'd been led to believe that my presence on set was on a need-to-know basis, which is why I'd kept schtum about the whole thing. Judging by the surprise on the three faces staring back at me, it looked like they'd been doing the exact same thing.

'Fancy seeing you here,' I smiled, settling myself in the vacant seat next to Bella.

'Likewise.' Bella's smile was bigger than mine. 'I'm glad you're here. We weren't sure, you see, that's why we didn't say anything.'

There was a moment of silence, in which we all just looked at one another.

'Win,' we said in unison.

'I can't believe she did that.' Suzie looked deflated.

'Really?' Deb scoffed. 'I can.'

Playing us off against each other. Smart move, Win. I decided to shrug it off. All of it. I was on a minibus that was about to take me to the first day of shooting for a TV series that would feature one of Britain's most talked about heartthrobs. If I was to let any of the previous night's conversation cloud my judgment, I'd be spoiling the opportunity of a lifetime. *I'll just use what the girls said to keep my wits about me, that's all.* When I thought about it, it was perfectly logical to have more than two wardrobe assistants on a job this size.

Any further discussion on the subject was cut short. Win climbed onto the bus and sat across the aisle. 'Hey, girls!' Her fake smile was firmly in place. 'Are we all raring to go?' Deb rolled her eyes and turned towards the window.

***

The first day started with a bang. The plan was to capture all the exterior battle sequences in just one day. When we reached the relevant field, in the middle of nowhere, it was already teeming with people—actors, extras, camera operators, sound crew, Make-up, Hair, Special Effects, set dressers...the list went on.

Once we left the bus, Win pulled us all to one side. 'Suzie, I've got you down to do wigs, so you best go and join Make-up.'

'Sure.' Suzie gave us a small wave and headed for the relevant trailer.

'Deb, Bella, I've got you working together on costume maintenance and order. I'm not entirely sure where our rails are at the present time, but I know they were in transit. Maybe your first task should be to track them down, so we can start dressing people.'

'Right,' said Bella. Deb nodded and they began their search.

'And Penny. Penny, Penny, Penny. I'm keeping you close to me today. I want you to have a front row seat for when the magic happens.' Win wiggled her index finger mysteriously.

'Okay.' I nodded politely. My instructions were rather vague compared to the rest of the girls'. Then again, it was my first day on set—maybe she was just being nice.

Most of the morning consisted of standing around in the cold at Win's side, whilst she dithered about and chatted to copious amounts of people. Eventually, she sent me for coffees. Bella's words from the night before rang in my ears, though I was kind of grateful for the task—at least it saved my fingers from dropping off with frostbite. As it got closer to shoot time, we joined Deb and Bella and began dressing some of the actors.

'Psst,' I hissed at Bella, who was working just a couple of feet away. 'Any sign of our star yet?' I was feeling rather giddy, but this could have been from a lack of food against a caffeine high.

I heard a little snigger leave Bella's lips. 'No,' she eventually whispered back as she waited for the next person to move towards her. 'But me and Deb both noted that all the lead's costumes were missing from our rails this morning.'

'They probably have their own trailers and dressers,' I supposed. Bella nodded as she helped an extra put on long socks.

'Speaking of missing, though...' Deb suddenly appeared from behind a rail. 'Where's Win?' We surveyed the dressing room. She'd slipped out during the commotion.

From Rags to Richie

'Probably gone to put Richie in his pants.' I knew I was being silly, but I couldn't help it. I'd hoped to at least set eyes on him again.

'That'll make a nice change for her,' said Deb, completely deadpan. 'I thought she only took those off her men.' Bella and I looked at each other, unsure how to react. 'Oh, lighten up, you two,' Deb said with a smile. 'I'm only joking. Even Win can't make long-johns sexy.' She pottered back to her own station as we tried to hide our giggles from the extras waiting in line.

Within an hour all the actors were dressed and on their markers. They listened intently to Craig as he talked them through the next few takes. Thinking back to my first opinion of him, Craig was a completely different man. The cold worked in his favour as his beanie covered his bald patch. His passion for the work showed; he was completely in his element. It knocked twenty years off him. By this time, I'd reconnected with Win, who gave no explanation for her absence. She silently watched Craig's every move, but I found it hard to concentrate. Now we were back outdoors the cold hit me all over again. *Note to self: wear warmer clothes to shoot days.*

'Richie, Richie, where are you?' Craig's shouts brought me to my senses. Richie Clarke emerged from the crowd. My word, that man is magnificent. I'd likened him to an oil painting that night in Carl's office; right now, he was verging on celestial. The uniform perfectly accentuated his physique. The long, blue tailcoat fit his tall yet slim frame perfectly. The tapering of the coat at his waist directed attention to his broad shoulders and athleticism. He stood proudly, as any war veteran rightly would. I began to feel weak at the knees.

'Penny. Penny?' I suddenly became aware of Win calling my name. *Oh God, how long had I ignored her? Shit.*

'Sorry! Got a bit engrossed in the moment there. Is everything okay?'

'You couldn't be a darling, could you, and fetch me another coffee? I feel like my toes are about to drop off.' She gave me one of her pleading smiles.

'Sure.' *Talk about poor timing.* I started to let out a sigh then caught myself. I was beginning to get a complex about the whole coffee runner thing.

Win added, 'Oh, if there's a bite to eat, could you bring that too, please? I'm famished.' On cue, my stomach made a loud rumbling sound. 'Looks like I'm not the only one,' she giggled before turning back to the crowd. Blushing slightly, I headed in the direction of the refreshments. I didn't take long as everyone was on set and not in the queue for the makeshift canteen. Still, by the time I returned, the war had begun.

I was gutted to have missed a magical moment—the beginning of it all. The reason we'd all put in so much effort and hours of our time. And Win had caused me to miss it. I glanced at her, but she just grabbed her food from me without so much as a thank you.

Chapter Nine

A couple of days later I decided to visit Aunt Ange at the shop. Initially, I thought it would be a nice surprise, given my suddenly hectic schedule. Filming was in full swing and in three days I'd already dressed more people than I had in my entire life. That afternoon had been devoted to a couple of interior shots with actors who were already in costume, so I was allowed a little time away, though Win said I needed to be back, full of energy, for the next day's more adventurous shots.

Aunt Ange had been eager to sit down for a chat, so much so that she even shut the shop for five minutes when I arrived. She gave me a hug and told me how proud she was of me, then handed me a hot drink and told me to spill all. Since filming had begun it had taken all my remaining energy to get back at night, eat, grab a shower, and get to bed. I had felt guilty not seeing Dad or Aunt Ange since all the fun stuff began.

I began filling her in on one of my favourite moments of the last few days. 'Win had to think fast on her feet and she ended up using the hot glue gun, of all things. Pulled it practically out of thin air, she did. And, using the tiniest amount of glue, she got the fabric to just the right point where it would hold up at the perfect angle. Genius.' I was gushing. But the way the costumes, actors and sets came to life so vividly, I couldn't help it. Plus, during the magical glue gun moment, I'd bumped into Richie—literally. He'd apologised to me sincerely for such a silly accident, he was so very sweet. Being so close to him, I could confirm that his denim jacket brought out the blue of his eyes. *Maybe that's why the glue gun moment sticks in my mind so?*

'Penny, what do you do exactly?' My aunt's eyebrows furrowed with concern.

Her question completely threw me. I didn't know what to say.

'Because I've heard all about Win, Suzie, Deb and Bella. And, of course, Richie Clarke. But nothing about my girl.'

I knew she was waiting for my answer, but how could I tell Aunt Ange, my fashion inspiration, that 'her girl' was only ever tasked with getting the big dog's coffee? In three days, it was becoming more and more apparent that 'Wardrobe Assistant' really meant assisting Wardrobe in getting their caffeine fix. *Perhaps I should reread the small print in my contract.*

'I'm a dresser.' That wasn't a complete lie; I'd jumped in and lent a hand to dress actors in some of the bigger scenes—like the battle scene on the first day.

'That's more like it. Penny, dresser of the stars.' I began to blush, and my aunt tutted when she saw. 'You need to believe in yourself more. Plus, I bet this Richie Clarke can't believe his luck, having a young girl like you with her hands all over him!' She winked.

I didn't think it was possible for me to blush any more than I already was, but somehow, I did, much to my aunt's delight. She let out a loud cackle before busying herself with her work.

***

Filming the following day involved a passionate rooftop scene. Huddled on top of the castle was a smaller crew, and I felt somewhat privileged that Win had called me to join her. I inwardly hoped that it wasn't so I could run up and down those steep castle steps to get her coffee. When I arrived, Richie and his leading lady, Millie Jones, were already in full costume. Craig wasted no time; as soon as the crew was in position, filming began. It was a wonderful scene to watch...the moment the two protagonists find they're unable to contain their burning desire for one another. *Aw, old school romance...*

A loud vibration emanated from our area during the first take. I looked over to see Win scrambling in her pocket to pull out her mobile phone.

'I've got to take this,' she whispered to me, and I gave her a thumbs up. The scene was in full swing, there wasn't much we could do anyway. However, after only a few seconds, Craig was on his feet.

'CUT!' Both actors jumped out of their skins. Millie immediately dropped the front of Richie's jacket and stepped away from him.

'Millie, darling.' Irritation permeated Craig's tone. 'Come here a second. Can I please remind you that you are compulsively, irrevocably in love with this gentleman?'

'Yes, I-I know, Craig.' Millie stumbled over her words.

'Then why are we not seeing it? Why are we not feeling it with your every move?' Mille looked like she wanted to the ground to open and swallow her up. 'We've got Richie Clarke here, three-time winner of *People* magazine's 'Sexiest Man Alive' poll. What more could you want?'

Richie opened his mouth to say something, but a glare from Craig silenced him.

'Right then. From the top.' Everyone shuffled back to their starting positions, but Richie began fumbling with his uniform.

'Wardrobe! WARDROBE!' Craig snapped. My stomach dropped. I looked around helplessly—Win was nowhere to be seen. It was either me or nothing. *Oh. My. God.*

'Sorry!' I could hear the crew mumbling as I rushed to where Richie stood. My palms began to sweat. His jacket was unfastened, and his shirt, dishevelled. He dropped his hands from the jacket buttons in defeat and gave me an awkward smile.

'I've never been good at dealing with buttons in a rush,' he muttered innocently, but my cheeks flushed at the connotation. He must have realised, too, because he avoided my gaze.

'And it was four times, by the way,' he added.

'Sorry?'

'Four-times winner of the 'Sexiest Man Alive' poll.'

'Oh.' I felt my stomach flutter again. 'Congratulations?' Oh, my life, kill me now!

'Er, thanks?' He shifted from one foot to the other. I smoothed the shoulders of his jacket down and stepped back to inspect my work.

'All done,' I said, smiling. Richie smiled back. He stood tall and proud, ready for a new take.

'Thank you,' he whispered before I scurried back to my place.

'And...ACTION!'

Phew! I did it. Watching the scene unfold again, I took a few steadying breaths.

Win returned. 'Did I miss much?' she whispered, slotting in beside me.

I shook my head. 'No, not really.' On the outside I wanted to act casual, but on the inside my heart was jumping around like a kid on a bouncy castle.

***

'Hello, excuse me!' The politest shout I'd ever heard followed me down the corridor of Shuderly Castle. Filming had wrapped for the day, and I was heading to Wardrobe to help Win prepare tomorrow's costumes. I turned round to see Richie jogging down the corridor, heading straight for me.

'Hey! It's Penny, isn't it?'

Richie Clarke remembered my name! I nodded.

'I wanted to thank you again for earlier and apologise for how much of an arse I must've sounded.' He chuckled awkwardly then combed his fingers through his beautiful brown hair.

It took me a few seconds to realise what he was talking about. 'Oh, don't worry about it.' I was surprised how casual I sounded, despite the fangirl inside me screaming with excitement. 'You were only stating a fact.'

He laughed again, a little more relaxed than before. 'Yeah, but I did sound a bit of a prick. I promise I'm not really like that.' We were interrupted by the ringtone on his phone.

'Shoot. Sorry, Penny, I've got to dash. See you around, yeah?' He headed back down the corridor.

'Bye!' I called after him, but he'd already gone.

Chapter Ten

'I'll have a flat white with a double shot, and Kim, Kim wants...KIM! What drink did you want again?' Sasha called out.

I was mortified to find myself, so quickly after my first proper costume job, in the middle of the make-up trailer taking yet more coffee orders.

'I'll have a gin and tonic,' Richie murmured from the dressing table, midway through being preened. There was a glint in his eye, and he was trying to hide a smile.

'I'll have a mocha.' Kim finally made an appearance from the back of the trailer, carrying a humongous powder brush.

'Ooh, I'll have a mocha,' Richie repeated in a sickly-sweet tone before grinning at me. At that, Kim launched the powder brush at Richie's face; it exploded into a cloud of white dust, forcing Richie to cough and splutter.

Laughter bubbled inside me, but I contained it. 'Sure thing, I won't be long.'

***

Later that day, we were given notice about some reshoots needed. As I helped Bella sort through the costume rails, Win appeared in the doorway.

'Penny! This is where you're hiding. Can I borrow you for a sec?' She chewed one of her long acrylic talons and looked around nervously.

'Sure. Is everything okay?' I asked, concerned. She didn't answer, she just grabbed my arm and led me out of the trailer.

Once outside, she looked around again before speaking quickly and quietly. 'I wouldn't normally ask this of you, especially with you being so new and inexperienced.' *Ouch!* 'It's a big responsibility and if I'm completely honest, I don't really trust anyone else to do it.' She took a deep breath. 'What I'm trying to say is, Craig is insisting on a late shoot tonight, but I can't make it. Will you step in for me?'

I blinked back at her. *Is this really happening?! Someone pinch me!*

'It's not a big job. In fact, it'll be an intimate crew. The only actors they need are Richie and Millie. But Richie's going to be in the water, so having someone from Wardrobe is crucial.'

My breath caught in my throat. Richie...in the water! Inappropriate images swam around my head.

'Honestly, Pen, this is really not like me. I have no choice.'

'I'll do it!' I said, shriller than intended.

'Oh, Penny, you're an absolute star!' I thought for a moment that she was going to hug me. 'Craig was filling me in earlier on the amazing work you did in my absence the other day. You dark horse, keeping that a secret! You must've made a good impression, he's more than happy to have you working with him tonight. Thank you so much, you were my only hope.' She smiled and visibly relaxed, as if the weight of the world had left her shoulders.

***

As the day began to wind down and people dwindled away from the castle, Win came to find me. In her hands she held the biggest bundle of keys I'd ever seen.

'These are for you.' She handed them to me with the utmost care. 'After shooting tonight, you'll escort Mille and Richie back to their trailers. These two keys are for that.' She held up two green topped keys from the bunch. 'Then you'll need to lock their costumes away, ready for tomorrow.' She held up a tiny key with a blue top. 'That's for the lead's wardrobe. Then you'll have to lock the costume trailer with this key.' That had a red top. 'Actually, Richie's costumes will probably need to go straight into the wash for Bella in the morning. Apart from that, I think that's it. Any questions?' I looked at the keys in my hand. *Trailers: green. Wardrobe: blue. Costumes: red.*

'Nope, I've got it, Win. You can count on me.' *Maybe this is the test I've been waiting for. Pass this and the sky's the limit.*

'I hope so.' Win didn't seem completely convinced. 'Don't show me up, now, I only want to hear good things in the morning.' She grabbed her coat and bag.

***

'Penny, hey! Nice to see you this fine evening.' As soon as Richie arrived on set, he flashed me one of his signature smiles. I instantly turned to mush. Behind him, in his director's chair, Craig rolled his eyes. Millie gave me a small wave as she passed.

'Everyone's here, Craig,' one of the techies called out from behind me.

'Brrrilliant.' Craig liked to roll his Rs. 'So, the plan is to get all the shots with Richie out the water first. Once he's in there, there's no going back. I need all hands on deck...he can only jump in once we're all happy.' There were murmurs from the crew. 'Once he's in, Penny, that's when I'll need you—the water will pull his clothes around. At the start of every retake, you'll need him looking sweet again. Is that okay?' I nodded enthusiastically. 'Grrreat. Right then...places, everyone.'

The scene involved Mille and Richie's characters acknowledging that they could not be together. The latter, Claude, was set to join the front line the following morning and Millie's character struggles to cope. She tries to talk him down and tensions run high, and he somehow ends up in the lake, looking sexier than ever as he tries to get away from her. She pulls him back and they share a mad, passionate kiss under the moonlit sky.

I'm glad I only help with the costumes, and I'm not involved with the script...

Things were straightforward to begin with. The

actors knew their lines and the crew knew their cues. Production was a well-oiled machine. I soon found myself kicking back and watching the story playing out before me. Because everyone was so professional, the water scene came quicker than I'd anticipated. In the dark, the lake looked like rippling oil. Richie was poised at the water's edge, ready to wade in. This was the shot everyone had been waiting for. We only had one chance at this, so it had to be right.

'ACTION!'

Off Richie went; he glided into the lake with precision and elegance. As soon as he hit the water, his white shirt billowed, clinging to him in all the right places. I felt a shiver run up my spine. As he waded further, his shirt, now sodden, became transparent. I was so proud of my department—this scene was going to make ladies drool.

On cue, Millie raced to the water's edge, 'Claude!' Richie turned to look at her, the water swishing around him beautifully, as if it was answering his command. It was poetic.

'Yes, my love?'

'Come back. Let me take you in my arms once more.' Millie reached out, as did Richie, water cascading from his sleeve. Their fingers were just a few inches apart.

'My dear, you know that cannot be. We said—'

'CUT! Guys, angles. Penny!' Craig called, jolting me from my daydreaming.

In I went. Richie waded over to the side of the lake, and I repositioned his shirt the best I could. I dusted off some of the debris that had stuck to him whilst the make-up girl adjusted his hair. He stood obediently as we worked. I locked eyes with him more than once; it was difficult to avoid doing so.

'Done,' the make-up girl and I called, in unison.

'Thank you,' Craig called back. 'Places, everyone, from Millie's first cry. ACTION!'

The moment played out again, and again, and again.

The fourth time I straightened his shirt, my fingers were shaking from the cold. Richie laughed. 'It's a bit nippy, isn't it?' His teeth chattered.

'Just a bit,' I replied, fumbling with a couple of his shirt buttons that had come undone. 'Millie's going to love it when you get out of here and give her a smooch.'

Richie laughed. 'She won't mind as long as it's done in one take. You can't please them all.' He winked up at me as I finished my adjustments.

'Oh, I'm sure you've got it in you,' I murmured back. I got on my feet and took my place behind the camera.

They went again. The way Richie marched over to Millie after he emerged from the lake... *Such strength, such power.* I was starting to understand why women loved period dramas.

'...AND THAT'S A WRAP, EVERYONE! Thank you.'

I ran to help Richie climb out of the lake. He was truly soaked. He still wore a smile on his face, even though I could feel he was shivering. I gave him a towel. Millie joined us; she was already wrapped up warm. I led them back to their trailers so they could get changed out of their sopping wet clothes.

Millie reappeared first, with a neatly stacked pile of towels and costumes. She gave me a kiss on the cheek. 'You did a fabulous job tonight, Penny. I'll let Win know all about it in the morning.'

'Thanks, Millie, that's so sweet of you,' I cooed, taking the pile of clothes from her arms.

'Don't mention it, I'm only telling the truth. Have a nice night.' She flitted off, into the arms of a man waiting for her at the gates of the castle.

Before long, Richie appeared, wearing only a towel. He held out a bag containing his wet costume. If I'd thought Richie looked gorgeous in the water, I hadn't prepared for this. His towel was precariously placed; I wished, I mean, I *thought* it might fall at any moment. His torso was broad and strong, with just the slightest suggestion of muscular definition around his abs. His damp hair was smoothed back, and his eyes twinkled in the moonlight.

'Penny? Are you okay?' Richie's face fell from a smile to a look of concern.

'Wow! I mean...s-sorry. Thank you.' I took the bag from him.

'Cheers. I won't be long.'

'No worries.' *Why am I stammering like an idiot?!* 'I'll just drop these off at Wardrobe and come back to lock up.'

'Cool.' Richie gave me a thumbs up before shutting his trailer door. It took every ounce of energy not to melt into the floor. *Get a grip, Penny, you're a professional.* Despite my self-scolding, I could not get the image of a topless Richie Clarke out of my mind.

In a zombie-like state, I headed over to the Wardrobe trailer; fumbling with the keys, I let myself in. Methodically, I placed Richie's clothes in the washing machine and placed Millie's costume back on the rail, ready for Deb's inspection in the morning.

As I went to leave, I caught a glimpse of some paperwork on the desk with my name on it. I moved closer and recognised Win's neat handwriting. At the top of the page was the heading 'Thursday' in block capitals. Below this was a list of tasks that I presumed would become tomorrow's concern.

1. Wash and dry Richie's costume
2. Dress extras for banquet reshoot
3. Reorganise rail
4. Discuss forward motions with Craig
5. Attend banquet shoot

It went on. Each point was allocated to a different person. Bella's name was down for washing Richie's costume, Deb was to reorganise the rails. My name did not appear until the very end of the list, next to the point that said 'Assistance', then (Coffee).

I wanted to scream. I could feel it brewing in the pit of my stomach.

Coffee! Coffee?! After I've covered for her tonight, she's still put me down for flipping coffee!

I stormed out of the trailer, banging the door shut and thrusting the key into the lock. Win had pissed me right off. I stomped down the steps then noticed Richie leant against the side of the trailer, waiting for me.

'I'm starving, aren't you?' he said. All I really wanted at that moment was my duvet, but my stomach had other ideas and let out a low rumble.

'My, my, the beast is alive!' Richie joked. 'Well, you can't turn me down now. Fancy a bite to eat?'

'Sorry, not right now.' My internal Aphrodite wanted to throttle me, but I couldn't help myself. I was so angry at Win's list that I wasn't in the mood to do anything other than go home.

But Richie didn't back down. 'I know, it will only be fast food at this ungodly hour, but at least it will fill the void. I promise we'll go somewhere a bit more reliable, not, you know, 'Kent's Tuck In Fried Chicken' or any of that nonsense.'

I walked past him to lock the door of his trailer and moved on towards Millie's. He followed me like a stray puppy.

'Richie, why are you being so nice to me? Most mega stars would have been long gone by now.' The words left my mouth before I could stop them. I wanted so badly to take them back.

He paused, but there was a smile tugging at his lips. 'Well, before, it was because I wanted to apologise for being a prick. But, if we've to work together more, ahem,' he coughed sharply, 'intimately, as we have done this evening, I'd at least like to take you out to dinner. Even if it is a McDonalds.'

I stopped in my tracks. *What is he doing? Why isn't he shouting at me or phoning Craig to have me dismissed for speaking to him like that?*

He continued. 'I think you've got a case of the 'hangrys'. I'm sure it's nothing a Happy Meal can't fix.'

I felt tears prick my eyes. Sometimes, I hated being a woman—a typhoon of hormones and emotional outbursts. I wasn't mad at Richie. I shouldn't have taken it out on him.

'I'm sorry, Richie, I didn't mean it.'

'I know,' he smiled. 'Come on, you can tell me all about it over lukewarm fries.'

I couldn't help smiling. 'Okay, you've twisted my arm.' I finished locking up and let him lead the way to the car park. My car would be safe enough at the office car park overnight, and I could always get the train in the morning.

Parked behind an FBW van was the fanciest car I'd ever seen. A classic black Mercedes Benz convertible, with alloy wheels, chrome everywhere and tinted windows. The sleek, shiny car was obviously Richie's pride and joy. It made my Vauxhall Corsa look like a toy in comparison. He pulled his keys from his pocket and the car lights blinked at us.

'Hop in,' he gestured, opening the passenger door. The interior was black leather with a walnut dash. It had the smell of a new car mixed with the whiff of expensive aftershave. Out the corner of my eye I spotted a baby's car seat in the back.

'Buckled up and ready to ride?' Richie smiled at me.

We fell into a comfortable silence, the radio filling the gap.

'Is this the real life? Is this just fantasy...?'

'Oh my god, I love *Queen!*'

'Really? I thought they'd be a bit...old for you?'

I threw him a look. 'Sorry, I didn't know there was an age restriction on good music?'

'No, I don't mean that, I'm actually impressed. I just wouldn't usually expect it from the younger generation.'

I wrinkled my nose. 'How old do you think I am?'

I saw him wince. 'I thought you were in your late

twenties. But I have this funny feeling you're about to tell me you've just turned eighteen and I'll have to turn this car round and take you straight home.'

'Richie!' I burst out laughing.

'What?! I'm just being honest. You can't be too careful.'

I shook my head. 'I'm twenty-seven-and-six-months.'

Richie gave a sigh of relief. 'Phew. I'm glad we've cleared that one up. That could have turned awkward.' He smiled at me before turning back to the road.

I began to hum along to the tune and, before long, Richie joined in. Humming led to singing and we were soon belting out the song, like we were in an episode of *Carpool Karaoke*. Harmonising beautifully, and taking it in turns to share the lines, the golden arches of McDonalds came into view.

'I see a little silhouette-o of a man!'

'Scaramouche, Scaramouche!'

'Will you do the Fandango?' Richie's eyebrows wiggled in time with the words.

'Thunderbolt and lightning...'

'Very, very frightening me!'

'Galileo!'

'Galileo!' Why he took the high notes, and I took the low ones, I'll never know.

'Gali-'

'Hi, can I take your order?' Richie jumped out of his skin, mid-Galileo. I burst out laughing. The poor woman on the other end of the tannoy didn't seem to share our amusement.

Our order served, Richie parked up and turned off his engine. We had a perfect view of the city lights twinkling. We'd not long left the picturesque landscape of the countryside; this view was just as beautiful.

'Come on, spill.' Richie tucked into his burger almost immediately, like he knew he was there for the long haul. The thought then occurred to me–as a husband and father of two, he was probably well practiced in the art of listening. It made a nice change–here was someone I could open up to, someone with the beauty of an outsider's perspective. I had nothing to prove to Richie Clarke; after this production was over, our paths would probably never cross again.

'I'm a glorified coffee runner, Richie. I honestly don't know what I'm doing here.' I put my head in my hands, my own burger completely forgotten. 'My family were so proud of me when I got this job...they're rooting for me to flourish. Now, when I go home, I'm either lying through my teeth about my work or telling them about Win's caffeine addiction.'

'You weren't a coffee runner tonight, though.' Richie popped a French fry in his mouth. 'I think you did a splendid job if I say so myself. Wardrobe maintenance, especially in water, can't be an easy task.'

'Tonight was a one off. I can't keep kidding myself.' I shook my head in defeat. 'When I left Wardrobe tonight, I spotted tomorrow's schedule on the desk. Win's only put me down for the coffee run. Again.'

Richie shook his head. 'Don't get so down on yourself, we've all been there. I've had my fair share of low-profile jobs: background characters, corpses, one-line speaking gigs that are often left to rot on the cutting room floor.' He chuckled, clearly reminiscing. 'It doesn't happen overnight, but it's all part of who we become. Your role is a step in the right direction, a foot in the door, the first rung of the ladder. One day, you'll look back and be grateful for this coffee run experience.'

Whether it was good advice, or whether it was due to feeling comfortable around him, I felt my anger subsiding.

Richie checked the clock on his dash. It was nearly two a.m. 'Oh my, I better get you home. Otherwise, neither of us will make it to set tomorrow, and people might start talking.' He winked before fastening his seatbelt.

On the journey home, I wanted to find out more about

Richie Clarke. I'd done enough talking for the evening. It was nice to sit back and listen, to let my overactive mind relax a little. Richie had a lovely voice, smooth and rich. His accent was that of an educated London gentleman with an extensive vocabulary–I could see why he'd done so much voice work in the past.

He told me about his two sons and how difficult it had been, adjusting to the Hollywood lifestyle, after they were born. Living Stateside for long periods of time, away from his kids, was one of the worst parts of the job, in his eyes. He never once mentioned his ex-wife or a partner. Still a sore subject, I guessed.

Richie spoke about the *Love and War* project, and how the comfort of a period drama drew him in. It was the kind of work he felt most at home with. He likened it to a huge tub of ice-cream, a cosy blanket, and a favourite film. *Could this guy be any more adorable?*

Before long, we pulled up outside my home. There was a huge part of me that didn't want the night (or, rather, morning) to end. I got out of the car and stooped to look at him through the open passenger window. His sharp features were enhanced by the shadows the low-light streetlamps created.

'Thank you for listening.' I beamed.

'Likewise.' Richie smiled back and held my gaze. His eyes really were the most beautiful shade of blue-green, even in the relative darkness. 'See you in the morning,' he said, his voice barely louder than a whisper.

A true gent, he kept the car gently purring at the kerbside until I was safely indoors, before driving off into the night.

Chapter Eleven

I woke up the next morning with a spring in my step. *Who wouldn't after spending an evening basking in the attention of Richie Clarke?*

I didn't see him for most of the day. I was called to assist with scenes that didn't involve him, and he never appeared in the coffee queue.

On my way to Wardrobe that evening, to collect my coat, I spotted Win talking to Richie behind the trailer. She let out one of her high-pitched cackles, which stopped me in my tracks.

'Oh, Richie, you do make me laugh!' She tapped his forearm flirtatiously.

'I'm just saying. Have a think about it, yeah?' Richie's grin matched Win's.

He then murmured something that made Win cry with laughter and toss her hair over her shoulder. It made me feel as if our 'date night' hadn't been so special after all. *That's showbiz, I guess...*

I dived inside the trailer quickly, hoping they hadn't spotted me. Looking to stall my departure, I ensured that there were no costumes on the floor; they were forever falling off their hangers or were often dumped by juvenile extras. Unfortunately, within a minute, I had the trailer spick and span.

Buttoning up my coat, I opened the trailer door and saw someone's toes on the steps. *Of course, it had to be Richie.*

'Penny! I'm glad I've bumped into you.' He wore ripped jeans and a white V-neck T-shirt; he was so effortlessly good looking, it was annoying. 'I really enjoyed last night. I think we should do it again sometime.'

I wondered whether celebs were pulled aside at the outset of their careers and trained to smile. Richie's grin was always perfect. No ugly laughter lines or dimply chin, just an even set of pearly-white teeth and a sense of happiness, demonstrated by the twinkle in his eyes.

'Sure.' I flashed him a fake smile while I finished fastening my coat.

He looked bemused. 'Could you be a little more enthusiastic?!'

'Look, last night…it was just two colleagues grabbing a Maccies, right?' I said, innocently.

He remained undeterred. 'Maybe we could try a nice steak rather than a burger. Are you free tomorrow evening?'

Was that an invitation for a date, Mr Clarke? For a moment, I didn't know what to say. *Had Richie Clarke, Megastar, just asked me, a coffee runner nobody from Wardrobe, out for steak?!* My female intuition was screaming loudly, reminding me that I'd just seen said celebrity megastar flirting with another woman. And that said woman just happened to be my boss, who supposedly had a track record for such behaviour.

What do I do?

I looked over Richie's shoulder and spotted Win. She was watching us from a short distance away, a look of snotty disbelief on her face.

I accepted Richie's offer. I had to agree with Win, as much as she frustrated me. I don't know how or why, but it seemed I'd hooked the big fish. Why not make the most of it? *Touché, Win, touché. I understand your concern, but I'm sure you'd do the same. This is Richie Clarke, after all.*

***

'They're not working you too hard, are they, love?' It was rare for Mum to be awake as I got ready for work. I yawned yet again. Richie had got my mobile phone number from somewhere and we'd been texting each other until the early hours.

'No, Mum. I'm fine, honestly.' We danced round each other in the kitchen as I made some lunch. 'I won't be home 'til late tonight.'

She threw her hands up. 'I hardly see you these days. You're up and out at the crack of dawn and not back until long after it's gone dark. Ange mentioned you're a dresser now. That's all very exciting, but please don't overdo it.'

'I won't, Mum, I promise. Something's just come up.' I gave her a kiss on the cheek. 'Don't wait up.'

How can I tell her I'm spending the evening with the star of the show? She'll have a list of questions a mile long!

I saw the look of disbelief on her face. I was a terrible liar, and she knew me too well. I just hoped she'd understand when she discovered the truth, whatever 'the truth' was.

***

'Do you do this often?' I asked candidly, as Richie took a large bite of steak.

He hadn't lied about stepping up our 'date night', if you could call it that. The steakhouse was gorgeous. There was an air of exclusivity and elitism—from the guest list, to how the staff acted when we arrived, as well as the fact that someone had valeted Richie's car. I'm sure I recognised the woman on table three from Saturday morning TV; this had to be a celebrity hotspot. But, no matter how lovely this place was or how handsome Richie looked in his steel blue suit jacket, or even that my steak was cooked perfectly, I'd never been one to beat around the bush—especially when it came to matters of the heart. *Once bitten and all that...*

His head bowed over his plate, he looked up at me with innocent, puppy-dog eyes. He calmly finished his mouthful before taking a sip from his wine glass. Then he dabbed the corner of his mouth with a napkin. 'Pardon?'

'I'm just curious,' I shrugged. 'A handsome gentleman like yourself, I just wondered whether this was a regular occurrence.' I turned my attention to my own plate and tried my hardest to emit a carefree persona.

'Well, I do try to eat three balanced meals a day. But with such a tight schedule, it can be difficult.' He had that playful twinkle in his eye again. I felt my heart flutter. *Dammit.*

'However, if you mean do I pick up girls from Wardrobe and take them for dinner in fancy restaurants, I'm afraid the answer is no.'

There was a pause. I wanted to say something clever or funny, but my mouth was uncomfortably dry.

'Of course, I have been known to wine and dine ladies at various points in my life. But as a recently divorced man, I'm not ashamed to admit that I'm a little out of my depth here.' Richie raised his hands, palms up, in surrender. 'How's your steak? Mine's delicious.'

I shook my head, still trying to comprehend his words. 'B-but, I thought...' I started. *God, this is embarrassing.*

Luckily, Richie seemed to be right on my wavelength. 'I know, famous guy, flashy car, star of the show... I understand. I'd be wary, too. Honestly, I'm not what the media portrays me to be.' He gestured to our lavish surroundings. 'As lovely as this is, I was just as comfortable in McDonalds. And, as for my divorce, I can either wallow in self-pity or get back out there. I'm just going with my gut right now.' He paused and looked at me with genuine concern. 'I hope I've not offended you. Because, if I have, we can leave right now. No harm done.'

'No, I'm fine. It's fine. More than fine, actually.' I took a moment to sip my wine and clear my head. 'It's just, like you say, your celebrity status precedes you.' I noticed him wince. 'And when I saw you talking with Win the other day, I just put two and two together...'

'And made five,' Richie finished. 'What you saw was Win talking at me. It happens a lot, actually. I actually thought it was part of her job description.'

'She certainly seemed to be lapping up your attention. All hair flicks and giggles.' I realised how immature I

From Rags to Richie

sounded. *Why does he make me so nervous?*

'Do I sense a hint of jealousy, Miss James?' His lips curved into a smile. He knew he'd hit the nail on the head. 'We were discussing my costume.'

'Yeah, right,' I scoffed.

'No, we actually were. There were a couple of design features I thought she might want to reconsider. She'd asked me for my opinion, so I gave it truthfully.'

I didn't answer, just raised an eyebrow. He sighed.

Lowering his voice, he leaned across the table and took one of my hands in his. 'Win is a very pretty lady, but she's just not my cup of tea. Like I said, I don't know what's happening here. But, as long as we're both having fun, I don't care about anyone else.'

So, if Win's not his type, does that mean I am? I didn't get chance to reply before a flash of light lit up the room.

'Richie, Richie!' a voice called out. 'Is it true your divorce cleared only a week ago and you're already on a date with another woman?'

Richie held my arm reassuringly as two restaurant staff wrestled the guy with the camera outside and pushed him towards the small crowd that had gathered. Our waiter ushered us through the kitchen doors and out the back entrance where, to my surprise, Richie's car and the valet driver were already waiting. *Had this been a setup?*

'I'm sorry, sir,' the waiter said, a pleading look in his eyes. 'We try our hardest to prevent this kind of incident at our restaurant. You and your guest have my sincerest apologies.'

Richie turned his back and grabbed his keys that were being offered by the valet. 'Just put the food on my tab.' His voice was gruff. As soon as my seatbelt clicked into place, Richie's foot hit the accelerator and we raced out of the restaurant car park before the paparazzi had chance to follow.

Time stretched on for what felt like a century with

neither of us saying a word. My heart raced and adrenaline pumped through my veins. *What just happened?* It had ended as quickly as it began. *Was this the reality of being with someone of celebrity status?* I'd thought it was thrilling, but I could tell Richie was pissed; his knuckles were white as they gripped the steering wheel.

I tried to make light of the situation. No one was hurt, it had just been a minor inconvenience. 'Well, that was new! Where's the next stop on our wild adventure?'

'I'm taking you home,' Richie said bluntly. There was no twinkle in his eye or playful smile, he just stared fixedly at the road ahead.

I thought about all the things I wanted to say in that moment—I wanted to take us back to the conversation we'd been having before the commotion. I wanted to ask him about what the paparazzi had said, if his divorce was really still that raw. But I didn't feel any subject appropriate amid the atmosphere.

Richie somehow managed to light a cigarette at the wheel. I didn't even know he smoked. Considering I got up close and personal with his clothes, he hid this well. Maybe it wasn't a habit he regularly indulged, just that tonight had thrown him. I decided to keep quiet and instead watched his wisps of smoke dance into the night.

Chapter Twelve

'Care to explain this?' Win thrust her phone in my face the minute I arrived at work the next morning. Her screen displayed a photo of Richie and me from the previous night.

'Don't worry, I've given Carl an excuse,' she said curtly. 'Told him it was strictly business, on my request. But you owe me. Spill.'

I didn't know what to say. I felt I should play it carefully, but I remembered her attempt to flirt with Richie and found it hard not to toy with her. 'It's what it looks like. He took me out for dinner.' I shrugged, a coy smile on my lips. 'It wasn't the first time. He's so sweet.'

Win pulled a face. 'It ends now.'

Wait, what?

'I can't have you messing this up for us, Penny. If that's what Richie needs, just leave it to the professionals.' She checked her lipstick and fluffed up her hair.

I couldn't stop the snort that came from me. *What made her so full of herself?* 'I don't think he's into you,' I muttered under my breath.

Win clearly had great hearing. 'Richie Clarke is no different to any of the other celebrity clientele I've dealt with,' she hissed through her teeth. 'He is not the gentle knight in shining armour you're making him out to be. He's a man with a big ego who's let fame go to his head. So back off and let the adults play.'

Woah. Was this 'Psycho Win' that everyone had warned me about? 'What makes you so sure?' I challenged.

'Just stay away from him. If you mess this up for us, there'll be hell to pay. And after this chat, I'll be the first to throw you under the bus.'

Before I had chance to respond, the rest of the girls arrived with their chirpy, excited energy. Win flipped like a switch and instantly joined in with their chitchat. Our discussion was over.

***

At lunchtime, Bella pulled up a seat next to me, her mobile phone in hand. It had been a hectic morning in Wardrobe, further exterior scenes had led to an onslaught of extras' costume maintenance. We'd barely had time to breathe, let alone talk to each other—although it had given me time to think things through.

'I didn't want to say anything in front of the others,' Bella began, a sheepish smile on her face, 'but I've got to ask, is this real?' She turned her phone and revealed the same photo Win had showed me.

The headline beneath read: *Richie Clarke Back on the Dating Scene with Mystery Girl.* Clearly, gossip travelled fast. They hadn't even bothered to find out my name.

I'd already decided that Win's threat meant nothing to me, but I didn't want to drag the girls into anything, especially if things were going to get messy.

'Oh gosh, not you as well!' I managed a fake laugh. 'It was just a costume meeting. Win sent me in her place because she couldn't make it.' I hated lying. Even small lies like that left a sour taste in my mouth.

Bella's shoulders dropped. 'Sorry, Penny, I should have known better. It's easy to believe gossipy journalism. They twist everything, don't they?'

I nodded solemnly.

'Still, I bet it was nice,' she said, smiling.

'He's a dreamboat,' I admitted, grinning back at her. We dissolved into a fit of giggles and chatted about other hunks over our tuna chunks.

***

I didn't catch a glimpse of Richie all day. When three days had passed and I hadn't seen him, I began to worry that he'd left the project and not bothered to let me know. Just as I was contemplating whether a missing person's report was necessary, he turned up at the Wardrobe trailer.

'Hey,' he said softly.

'Sorry, do I know you?' I shot him a puzzled expression.

'Come on, don't be like that.' He was wearing his signature lopsided smile, the one that obviously led to him winning the 'Sexiest Man Alive' award four times in a row. *Or was it five? Focus, Penny, focus.*

'Am I supposed to pretend that you haven't been avoiding me these past few days?' I turned towards the table, but he just walked around it and perched his 'Rear of the Year' on the edge. 'Mixed signals, much?' I murmured.

'My agent advised me to not be seen with you, for a while at least. With the press coverage and all. Throw them off the scent, that kind of thing.' He paused, his eyes scanning me for a reaction. I kept my head down. 'I presumed Win would've told you to do the same. It's fairly routine in these situations...' He trailed off. 'I'm being an egotistical celebrity again, aren't I?' He rubbed the back of his neck, sheepishly.

I finally looked at him and raised my eyebrows. 'Never has anyone given me a strategic battle plan to outsmart the media, and never have I needed one...until now.'

In one last ditch attempt to charm me, he said, 'Opposites attract?'

It worked and I blushed profusely. I could've kicked myself.

'How about I make it up to you, with an invitation for a second date?' He leaned towards me until our faces were mere inches apart.

'Isn't that exactly what we shouldn't be doing? It's only been, what, three days since my gossip column debut?'

Richie batted my concerns away with a wave of his hand. 'I've got a plan. Pick you up tomorrow night?'

Richie Clarke, you beautiful yet complicated being. Of course I wasn't going to say no. To hell with Win's threat. I couldn't turn down a second date with Richie Clarke, even if we did run the risk of being chased by the paparazzi again.

'Brilliant. That's settled, then.' He flashed his Hollywood

smile. 'Oh, and mind if I borrow this?' He reached past me and grabbed a spare shirt from the rail. I caught his woody cologne, and it sent my head reeling. So much so, I didn't realise he'd taken his shirt off. He replaced it with the one from the rail.

'What?' he looked at me innocently. 'It would be highly suspicious if I returned empty handed, wouldn't it?' He smiled, the twinkle in his eye again.

'See you tomorrow, Penny,' he called as he left.

Chapter Thirteen

The following evening, Richie pulled up in his Mercedes Benz to collect me for our second date and my stomach did a little somersault. He had the top down and the soft, mellow sounds of *The Eagles* drifted through the autumn evening air.

'Hey,' he said softly.

'Hi.' I couldn't help but take note of his attire. Normally, I saw him in period costume—consisting of shirts, blue coats, and long johns. This evening, he wore skinny jeans, a grey hoodie and Nike trainers. He looked younger, trendier. It was not what I'd expected him to wear, but he looked good. I tugged at the hem of my plaid jumpsuit, suddenly feeling overdressed.

'Ready?' Richie asked.

I nodded. 'I like your outfit, by the way. Nice treads.'

'Thanks.'

Before long, we pulled into the car park of his hotel.

'Welcome to my humble abode,' he joked as he opened my door.

The hotel was as I'd expected, lavish and extravagant. I wondered how much of *Love and War's* budget had been spent on accommodation alone. To my surprise, we didn't head to the hotel restaurant or the bar. Instead, Richie guided me to the lifts, and to his room. Once inside, he took my coat and hung it on the back of the door.

'Wine? Gin? Beer?' He gestured to the mini bar.

'Umm...rosé, please.'

'Coming right up.' Richie took the bottle from the fridge and poured me a glass. I'd always been under the impression that drinks from a mini bar had to taste exceptional, given their ridiculous price tag, and I wasn't disappointed. The rosé was ice cold, fancifully sweet and very refreshing. Richie opted for a gin and tonic.

'I wanted to bring you somewhere more private this time. I hope that's okay.' He sat down on the large double bed, which took up most of the room. He paused before adding, 'Not too forward, I hope?'

If I thought I had nervous butterflies before, right now I felt I must have a congregation of anxious alligators in my stomach.

'No, no. I understand. It's actually rather nice,' I replied, trying to keep my cool. 'Don't get me wrong, fancy restaurants are great...' Richie gave me a small smile. '...but I like the privacy of a room. No prying eyes.' I instantly realised how that must have sounded. 'And the additional space, of course.'

Richie let out a small laugh and patted the space beside him, inviting me to join him on the bed. I paused but eventually obliged, after my stomach did another giddy turn. I took another sip of wine to steady my nerves.

Something in the air seemed to have changed. Everything seemed soft and gentle, more sensual. I wasn't with 'Richie Clarke, three times BAFTA winner' tonight. There wasn't the paparazzi lurking around every corner. It was just Richie, me, and the mini bar. I liked that.

We ended up talking about nonsense—everyday things— from our favourite foods and restaurants to our most watched films and TV shows.

'I'm more of a thriller man if I'm honest. Reservoir Dogs, Silence of the Lambs, Dexter, that sort of thing,' said Richie.

I raised an eyebrow. 'So, what you're saying is you would never watch something like...oh, I don't know, *Love and War?*'

Richie squirmed a little and I burst out laughing.

I could feel the wine going to my head. Maybe drinking multiple bottles from the mini bar had been a bad idea, but Richie had just kept topping up my glass. Our conversation had fallen into a natural lull, and at some point, we moved from a seated position to lying down on the bed next to each other. The alcohol must've affected

Richie too; he began humming away to himself and even conducted an invisible orchestra. I recognised the tunes and was just happy to listen; I soaked up the atmosphere and simply enjoyed the mix of sensations.

'I like you.' The words slipped out of my mouth. No premeditation, no build up. I didn't regret them, and I wasn't embarrassed, it was the truth. It was exactly how I felt in that exact moment. The words hung in the air. The longer the silence stretched on, the more immature my utterance sounded. I inwardly kicked myself for saying such a silly thing. Awkwardly, I added, 'After our recent episode with the media, and with Win and everything else, I just wanted you to know that.'

Richie let out a small laugh. I looked at him, suddenly panic-stricken that he was laughing at my feelings.

'I like you too,' he said breathily. For a split second my brain stopped functioning entirely.

I rolled onto my side, and he copied me. For a few seconds we just stared at one another.

He propped himself up on one elbow to bring his face level with mine. I inhaled sharply. *Oh my god, he's going to kiss me!* I hadn't prepared for this. His lips drew closer, his head tilted, and I closed my eyes. I couldn't believe this was about to happen. *I was going to kiss Richie Clarke!* But the moment never came. I waited an extra heartbeat, in case I was jumping the gun a little, but still nothing. I felt him move on the bed and I opened my eyes.

'Sorry, Pen,' he sighed, defeated. 'I want to. I really do. But we just can't.' He swung his legs over the edge of the bed and put his head in his hands. 'I'm sorry I led you on,' he mumbled. 'This is for the best, I promise. And I know, deep down, you agree.'

He turned to face me, looking utterly crestfallen. 'My divorce feels raw. Hell, a couple of weeks ago, I almost pulled out of this project entirely, because I couldn't handle coming back to work and leaving the boys—and to act out a love story, for Christ's sake! It would be cruel of me to sweep you up into this whirlwind when I don't really know what's going on myself. I'm being entirely selfish; I knew it as soon as I left you the other night. My feelings for you were growing stronger than I'd anticipated. Then that whole thing with the paparazzi...I took it as a sign. So, I made the decision to keep away from you, it wasn't because my agent told me to. I was trying to save us both some heartache. But I couldn't even keep away from you for a week. How embarrassing is that?'

I wanted to react, to tell him it was okay, and that we could take each day as it comes. I wanted him to know that I didn't care about the chaos. Before I could respond, he put his finger to my lips and stopped me in my tracks.

'You deserve better than someone on the rebound, Penny.'

My gut was telling me to get out of there. If that was how he felt, then I shouldn't waste my time. *Don't give him the privilege. This is Richie Clarke, remember...he's had tons of women throwing themselves at his feet. Don't be another one, Penny James.* But there was another side of me that cared for him, that had recognised truth in everything he'd said, who believed he was looking out for me. *What should I do? Walk away, or try and persuade him otherwise?*

'If it's for the best, what more can I say?' Richie's eyes widened. He'd obviously expected a different reaction. I'd shown maturity. Stayed matter of fact. Opted to be drama-free. *Mission accomplished.* 'Well, if that's decided, you can at least pour me another drink,' I said, holding up my glass.

He fumbled slightly as he took it from my hand. 'Of course, that's the least I can do.'

'To star-crossed lovers.' I raised my glass in a mock-toast then threw back more wine. He watched me like he was studying a bomb, expecting it to explode any second.

'Are you okay?' he asked gently.

'I admit, I've been better. But there's no use crying about it, is there? Come on now, leave me with some dignity.' Richie still looked at me with concern. 'I understand you've had a lot on your plate recently. I'm sure you'd rather me be a shoulder to cry on than your sworn enemy.'

Silence fell. We both seemed to be processing what the other had said. I felt weirdly proud that I'd taken the high road. I stole a glance at Richie; he was looking down into his glass, his face expressionless. I wondered what he was thinking.

'Oh, sod it.'

In a flash, Richie threw his empty glass down and took my face in his hands. Before I could react, we were kissing each other. At first, I didn't know what to do. I was actually kissing Richie Clarke, something I hadn't been able to stop thinking about since I first laid eyes on him. Nature soon took over and I pushed my body against his, giving in to my desire. My hands moved to Richie's waist, and I snaked them around him, deepening our kiss further. I heard him give a gentle groan as he shifted slightly and swung me onto his lap.

After a few seconds, I had to break away. Begrudgingly, because I definitely didn't want it to end. I caught my breath and looked up at Richie, whose face was flushed.

'So, about that little speech before,' he began.

Now it was me pressing my finger against his lips. 'I understand, Richie. Baby steps.'

He laughed softly and nodded. 'Baby steps.'

'If it works, it works. And if it doesn't, well…at least we'll have had fun.' I tried to sound as carefree as possible. Richie was grinning, it was adorable. I suddenly remembered Win's threat. 'It's probably best if we keep this to ourselves for now, though. Agreed?'

'Most definitely.' He leaned in for another kiss, and then another, and another—until I had to push him away, giggling all the while.

'I best get going,' I whispered. If I didn't go, I feared my lips would drop off. Plus, I'd promised Mum I wouldn't be too late.

'Do you have to?' Richie let out an exaggerated sigh as I brushed his fringe to the side. 'You're welcome to stay here tonight. You'd have a five-minute drive to work in the morning—chauffeur driven, of course. A cosy lie-in with yours truly?' He winked at me and lounged back on the bed suggestively.

'As tempting as that is, would that not completely give the game away?' I asked, against my better judgement. Celebrity or not, I reasoned, if I wanted whatever this was to be more than a one-night stand, he'd have to work for it.

After a few seconds spent contemplating, he simply nodded. 'Baby steps.' He got up from the bed and reached for his coat.

'Where do you think you're going?' I asked, as Richie fumbled around for his keys.

'If you're not staying here, I need to take you home, silly.' Almost on cue, he wobbled and nearly lost his footing.

'No, you don't, mister. Not in that state.' I guided him back to the bed. 'The best place for you right now is here.' Initially, he succumbed, but then he shot back up.

'I'm not having you travelling back alone.'

'Richie, don't worry, I'll get a taxi.'

'Let me call you a cab.' He lunged towards his phone, knocking his tumbler flying in the process.

'Okay, fine. You can call me a cab.'

Richie smiled and unlocked his phone. Within seconds, a taxi was booked. 'I've got a lot of respect for you, Penelope James,' he said, lifting his hand to trace my cheekbone with the tip of his thumb.

'Goodnight, Richard Timothy Clarke.' I broke away from his touch and started down the hotel corridor.

'Huh?'

I couldn't resist turning back and giving him a wink before rounding the corner for the lift. 'Sweet dreams!' *Oh, the powers of Google. That man has so much to learn!*

When I got to the foyer, my taxi was already waiting. The driver was so kind, jumping out to open the back door for me, offering to put my bag in the boot, asking if I minded him playing his music on the radio. I swear that celebrities had an elite phone book—I wouldn't normally receive such treatment.

As we arrived at my front door there was only one thought in my mind: I was officially on kissing terms with Richie Clarke.

Chapter Fourteen

The following weeks were a blur of stolen kisses and secret moments. No other soul knew what was going on between us (not even my mother). I admit, it was exciting.

Richie's trailer quickly became my second home. When I first stepped through the door, I couldn't believe it. The other trailers were stuffy at best, but his was like a five-star hotel. It even had a bed and sofa. Miraculously, I'd also been allowed to assist (and I mean *actually* assist) on more shoots. I knew this was down to Richie whispering in Craig's ear, but I wasn't complaining. I was having the time of my life, getting to undress Richie all day. I could tell that my sudden 'promotion' riled Win. She'd given me a few sharp looks and a bit of the silent treatment as well. She preferred me as a coffee runner rather than a colleague.

The only problem was that our time together, during breaks and after long shoots, wasn't long enough. It was getting harder and harder to slip away unnoticed, particularly with Win on high alert. But I couldn't deny that it was the cheeky winks, the sideways glances, the whispered compliments, and the overall thrill of our secret affair that got me up in the mornings.

One day, I was drinking my morning coffee in the Wardrobe trailer and having a much needed catch up with Bella, Deb, and Suzie when Richie appeared in the doorway.

'Sorry to interrupt, ladies,' he said. Suzie turned a deep magenta. 'Am I right in thinking it's castle interiors today?' Bella nodded enthusiastically.

Deb took a suit bag from a wardrobe rail. 'Yes, including the ballroom scene. I've been waiting to catch you; I need to make sure all my alterations are finished

From Rags to Richie

on this. Have you got a few minutes?'

'Sure.' Richie shot me a mischievous grin as he passed.

Suddenly, there was a topless Richie Clarke in our vicinity. Poor Suzie didn't know where to look. She tried to busy herself and got redder and redder by the second. Richie's physique was a sight to behold—slim yet strong with an athletic frame. I had to stop myself from drooling. He was a sex god and there was no denying it.

Deb worked quickly, shortening cuffs, pulling in this, tightening that. I could only dream of being as speedy and efficient as her. Within minutes, she was done.

Richie approached me while buttoning up his shirt. 'Penny, would you be able to bring this costume over to my trailer when Deb's finished with it? I wouldn't normally ask something so mundane, but I'm afraid I've got to dash. I better not keep Craig waiting any longer.' Richie mimed his throat being slit and a dramatic death face. Suzie snorted.

'No problem,' I smiled. When the others weren't looking, I winked at him over the brim of my coffee cup.

'You're a star.' He leaned over and placed his hand on my shoulder in gratitude—longer than was appropriate, though I don't think anyone paid any attention. He waved to us all. 'Bye, ladies.'

'Bye,' Suzie said, meek as a mouse.

Maybe it was because I knew him better by now, but it was funny to see the effect Richie had on other women. As soon as he left, Bella fanned herself. Suzie slowly returned to her natural colour, and Deb meticulously refolded a pile of costumes into a neat stack.

'Come on, ladies, it was only Richie Clarke, five-times winner of the 'Sexiest Man Alive' award,' I said. The three of them pulled a face before we burst into laughter.

I arrived at Riche's trailer, costume in hand. He answered almost immediately.

'Ta-da!' I held the costume up for him to admire Deb's handiwork.

'That was quick.' He let me in and locked the door behind me.

'I know, right? When it comes to sewing, no one's better than Deb.' I took my time laying out the costume on Richie's bed, wiggling my bottom in his direction as I did so. Before he had chance to react, I straightened myself and pounced on him.

He leaned into my kiss. I wrapped my legs around his waist, and he carried me across the trailer to his desk, where he put me down. He attempted to talk between my kisses.

'Though I love this, there is something I want to ask you. I need a teensy, weensy favour.'

I released him from my grasp and leaned back slightly to look him in the eye. He cleared his throat. *What could he possibly have to say? Did he want to tell the crew about us? Did he want me to stay with him at the hotel for the rest of the shoot?*

'Can you dance?'

Can I dance?!

My knee-jerk reaction was to laugh, but after noting the serious look on his face, I opted for a raised eyebrow.

'You know that Deb said it was the ballroom shoot this afternoon? Well, I could really do with practising my waltz.'

I tried my hardest to stifle a giggle. He was being serious—he genuinely wanted my help.

'Richie, I don't think I'm very good –'

'Nonsense,' he interrupted. He got up and began to move the sofa against the trailer wall. 'For girls it's easy, as long as you have a strong lead.'

'And do I?'

He paused. 'That's what we're about to find out. I'm either a natural or I've been born with two left feet. You should have seen my first dance at my wedding.' He grimaced. 'No wonder she divorced me.' He cleared his throat again and there was emotion in his voice. *It's clearly still raw.*

Taking my hand, he moved his other to my waist and pulled me close. The sudden movement made my breath catch in my throat. He gazed down at me, and I felt as though I could melt into a puddle at his feet.

There's something very sexy about dancing. In the animal kingdom, it's an integral part of many mating rituals. Peacocks, for example, attract their mates by shaking their booty. *Not dissimilar to the average Saturday night up town, not that I'd have much of a clue about that.*

As Richie and I swayed and twirled around his trailer, I transcended to another realm. We were in such close proximity that our bodies moved as one. I didn't just take his lead, I felt it.

Too quickly, the song on Richie's mobile came to an end. As a finishing move, he spun me out to his right and gave a small bow.

'You lied about having two left feet.'

'I told you, it was a fifty/fifty gamble.' There was that mischievous glint in his eye again.

***

'CUT!' Craig shouted, hopping out of his director's chair. 'That'll do for tonight, folks. I'll see you all in the morning.'

Win immediately started barking orders to the cast about where to deposit their costumes. My eyes drifted over to Richie, who wasn't listening and was instead whispering something to Millie. He must've felt me watching him because he turned to look right at me.

The ballroom sequence had been mesmerising. Cast and crew had worked together seamlessly to bring the moment to life. It was probably my favourite scene of the whole production—discounting Richie's water scene, of course, for obvious reasons. I gave him a thumbs up and he grinned.

Win marched in the direction of Wardrobe and I scurried after her. 'Penny, there you are.' She didn't even look at me when I caught up. 'As soon as the main cast's costumes are checked in, you can get off home.'

'Oh.' I was slightly thrown. Over fifty costumes had been used in the evening's shoot, surely Win wasn't going to tackle all that by herself. 'Are you sure? I don't mind staying.'

Win shook her head. 'I've got it covered.'

Richie and Millie returned their costumes relatively quickly, so it took me barely any time to lock everything up. When I took the garments to the Wardrobe trailer, Win was amid a sea of costumes. Deb was helping her.

'Hey, Deb. I didn't realise you were still here.' She shot me a small smile as she hung costume after costume on the various rails.

'Bye, Penny.' Win sounded irritated. 'See you tomorrow.'

'Bye then.' I left the trailer and forced my way through the crowd of extras returning their costumes. I spotted Richie lingering.

'I'm all done,' I said.

'Well, I'm in no rush to get back.' He lit a cigarette and turned to face the magnificent castle. 'Fancy immersing yourself in a bit of culture?' He offered me the crook of his arm. We were mere centimetres from the costume trailer that was heaving with cast and crew. It was so dangerous, but I couldn't help myself.

'Don't mind if I do,' I said in my best posh accent. I took his arm graciously. We giggled quietly, like a couple of teenagers, happy to be alone with each other.

We reached the museum section of the castle and were greeted by one of the castle's security guards.

'I can give you, like, an hour, max,' he mumbled.

'Thank you. That's perfect.' Richie smiled at the guard then led me through a large stone archway.

'What was that all about?' I asked, bemused.

'I may have cut the fine gentlemen a deal.' There

From Rags to Richie

it was, the Richie eye twinkle. 'His mum is a big fan. A five-minute video call has granted us an hour of freedom in a paparazzi-free environment.'

'Oh, Richie, you didn't have to do that.' I felt giddy.

'I know, but it was actually quite fun,' he chuckled. 'Bless her heart, the poor woman was ready for bed. She had her rollers in and everything. I gave her the shock of her life.'

On the walls of the first room hung paintings of the aristocracy that had lived there throughout history, as well as various artists' impressions of what the castle used to look like. Dimmed spotlights had been strategically placed to illuminate information, but also to give the illusion of candlelight. I ran my fingers along a wall; its surface was rough and cold to the touch. I was lost in a daydream—it was as if the castle belonged to me and Richie. In my mind, I walked the long corridors in excessively puffy dresses and tiaras, and he wore a pair of tights. He even looked good in *them.*

As I was fantasising, Richie wandered into the next room. I eventually walked through the second stone archway and found him scrutinising a miniature replica of the castle grounds. Despite being a model, it consumed most of the room, in both size and grandeur. Richie concentrated on its intricacies, his hand resting on its information plate.

I moved behind him and snaked my arm under his, running my fingertips down his wrist. I traced along his long fingers and circled his knuckles tentatively, before curling my fingers around his and taking his hand in mine. Richie turned to face me. His other hand cupped my face. Without a second's thought about being seen, I instinctively closed the gap between us and kissed him softly. The next thing I knew, my lower back was pressed up against the glass of the castle miniature. Richie's tongue slid over my bottom lip and the kiss deepened. Our tongues danced and swirled together as our hands roamed each other's bodies. We were quite provocative, to say we were in a museum. My senses surrendered—my passion for Richie ruled me entirely.

Suddenly, we heard a cough from the other side of the room, and we jumped apart like we'd had a bucket of ice-cold water thrown at us.

It was the security guard, looking rather sheepish. He spoke in gruff voice, not quite making eye contact with either of us. 'Sorry to, ahem, intrude. I have to lock up now.'

Was Richie blushing? It was hard to tell in the dingy room. 'Oh, sorry,' he said. 'Thank you. We'll be on our way.'

Embarrassed, I raised a hand in gratitude to the security guard as we slipped out. We hurried down the stone steps, out of the castle doors and into the night. *Note to self: don't give in to temptation so easily, regardless of how hot Richie Clarke may be. Practise self-restraint.*

'Do you think he'll tell anyone?' I clung to Richie's arm, bracing myself against the bitter wind.

'No, I'll have a word with him tomorrow. Introduce him to my good friend, Liz.' Richie lifted the corner of a twenty-pound note from his blazer pocket then tucked it back inside.

'Richie! You can't go around bribing people.'

He shrugged, unfazed. 'What? Money talks. Or not, in this case. Trust me, you've got nothing to worry about.' He bent to give me a peck on the lips. We'd been so brazen; we were still on FBW territory. But in that moment, it hadn't mattered.

I tapped his arm playfully but kissed him back all the same. 'Whatever am I going to do with you? You're such a bad boy.'

'Don't you prefer me that way?' He scooped me into a fireman's lift without warning. He carried me across the car park to his car as I squealed with laughter.

As Richie drove us out of the complex, I mindlessly looked out of the window, across the makeshift village of trailers. My eyes fell on Wardrobe, and I let out an exasperated sigh.

'What's up?'

'Oh, nothing. It's just someone's left the light on in the Wardrobe trailer.'

'Do you want to go back and deal with it?'

'No. How would we explain being together? And I clocked off over an hour ago.'

A playful smile graced his lips. 'Either that or you're getting paid to kiss me. But don't worry, darling, you wouldn't be the first.'

I shoved his arm playfully and we both laughed as he drove out of the gates. I was too distracted to notice that the light in Wardrobe had just that moment been turned off.

Chapter Fifteen

A couple of hours into the morning, Win caught me as I was ironing some costumes for the afternoon shoot. 'Penny! Just the person I wanted to see.' Win had her fake smile plastered across her face. I felt queasy. 'Something's come up. I need you back at the office.'

'Oh.' That wasn't what I'd expected her to say. My shoulders slumped, but I tried to conceal my disappointment. 'Sure. What do you need me to do?'

'There's a list on my desk. Just work through as much of it as you can. Ciao!' She scampered off without looking back.

Deflated, I trudged through the grounds to my car. At the office there would be no costumes, no lights, no action...no Richie! Once there, in the middle of our desk, I found the humongous pile of papers stacked neatly. I let out a pitiful groan. *Was it too late to pull a sick day?*

A few hours later, as I was still trying to make headway through the paperwork, my mobile vibrated on the desk. A message from Richie came on the screen.

Hey, where are you hiding?

I looked round the empty office and sighed. There were other people somewhere in the building, but I felt quite alone in that room.

Win's got me trapped at the office today. I'm currently buried under a paper Mount Everest.

There for the long haul, huh? That's a shame. I miss you.

I felt butterflies flutter in my stomach. *He missed me!*

I miss you, too. I should reach the summit by sundown. See you tomorrow?

There was a slight delay in his response. In fact, I'd assumed he'd put his phone down and gone back on set, but then my phone vibrated again.

Yes. Hopefully, it's just a blip. See you tomorrow.

I realised that this was the first day since we'd got together that I hadn't seen him—and that sucked. It was crazy how quickly my feelings had grown, almost scary. In a bid to think of anything but Richie, I picked up the next sheet from the top of my paperwork pile: an invoice for eight rolls of elastic. I filed it away in the relevant folder and picked up the next: a receipt for twenty spools of extra strong thread. Admin was such a bore.

About an hour later my phone vibrated again. I scrambled for it frantically, hoping that it would be Richie. This time, Suzie's name appeared.

Hey, we've all missed you today! (Even Richie was asking for you earlier!) Win told us you had some admin to catch up on, which totally sucks. Hopefully you'll be back with us in the thick of it tomorrow! Fancy dinner with us tonight so we can fill you in on the day's shenanigans?

Suzie was so sweet, she always thought of others. A proper catch up with the Wardrobe girls was long overdue.

Sure. Can't wait!

***

The pub was packed, but we managed to grab a table outside the ladies' toilets. Classy. I don't think any of us minded, though, we were too famished to notice. Conversation didn't really start until our mains arrived.

It quickly turned to work. Luckily, it didn't sound like I'd missed much. Filming had mainly involved interior shots with the main cast and few costume changes. The girls had busied themselves with costume repairs and maintenance instead.

'I'm surprised I made it on time if I'm honest,' Deb yawned. 'Last night was a late one.'

'What time did you leave?' I asked.

'Just after you. About fifteen or twenty minutes later.'

Did Deb see me go into the castle with Richie?

'Oh, I didn't leave straightaway,' I said, blushing slightly. 'I had some, um, other business to attend to. I left about an hour after that.' I tried to keep my voice level, carefree.

'Yeah, I know. I saw you go. I was finishing some of the bits and bobs Win left.' Deb sounded casual, but her stare was cold and hard. I felt my blood turn to ice. *She saw us. She probably also saw him carrying me to his car.*

Act casual.

'When I left, I thought someone had left the trailer light on. I nearly came back and turned it off.' I smiled at her as I tried to play it cool. I felt the conversation was getting too close for comfort—I was practically squirming in my seat. I'd have to warn Richie.

'Yeah, it was me in there. I could tell it was you outside, I recognised your laugh.' *Dammit. How do I explain away what the others would assume was me laughing to myself?* I'd have to either admit that I was with someone, which could lead to some awkward questions, or claim insanity. I was about to opt for the latter when Deb got up. 'I'd better get off, ladies. I'm still exhausted from last night, and I don't want to risk being late in the morning.' She stifled a yawn before saying her goodbyes.

I needed a breather. I also needed to speak to Richie. 'I'll just be a second,' I said, heading to the toilets. As soon as I walked through the door, Deb emerged from one of the cubicles. I jumped out of my skin.

'I was hoping you'd come in here,' Deb's smile was softer than earlier. She washed her hands then wrapped her arm around my shoulders.

'I'm sorry, Penny. I know we're friends, but I couldn't let it happen again.' She paused. 'I need this job, and I deserve a promotion. I've worked here for five long years—it wouldn't be fair if another young thing in a short skirt got in the way. Whatever happens between you and Richie is your business, I'm not going to go around shouting it from the rooftops. But I'm putting my armour in place. Perhaps you should lay low at work for a couple of days until it all blows over. I needed to make sure that you weren't clouding anyone's vision. Sex is a powerful weapon, Penny. One day, you'll understand.'

I was gobsmacked. *What had she done? Who had she told?* My hands began to tremble at my sides. I wanted to say something, but I was too scared. If I reacted, the cat was definitely out of the bag. If I stayed silent, she had nothing to go on, apart from what she thought she'd seen. No concrete evidence. I suddenly remembered the security guard at the castle. *Oh God, I hope they didn't bump into each other last night...*

'I'm going now.' Deb made her way to the door. 'I'll see you in the morning.'

'Goodnight, Deborah,' I said through gritted teeth.

What just happened? I splashed my face with cold water, trying to compose myself, and smartened myself up in the mirror. When I returned to the table, Suzie and Bella were eyeing up the dessert menu. I was relieved that they were in no rush to get home.

'I'm torn between the warm chocolate fudge cake and the salted caramel cheesecake,' sighed Suzie.

'Ooh, that's a hard choice. I'm leaning towards the lemon meringue,' said Bella.

I settled in my seat, trying to appear cool and calm, as if nothing had happened. I picked up the menu but couldn't focus on a word of it.

'Guys...' I started. They both looked up from their menus. Maybe they'd detected the slight tremor in my voice, or the obvious change in atmosphere; I felt like they already knew what was coming.

'Can I ask you a question? I know that Deb doesn't trust Win because she stole her promotion, but is there more to the story?'

Bella rolled her eyes. 'You better get the desserts in,

Suzie. It's going to be a late one.'

By the time Suzie made it back to the table, desserts in hand, Bella was already in full swing. 'So, Deb was one of three girls who started in Wardrobe at FBW Productions when the company was young and small scale. Everything was low budget at that time: tomato ketchup for blood, talcum powder for grey hair, that kind of thing. Eventually, the other two women moved on to bigger and better things, but Deb stuck with the FBW team...and Carl in particular—they started seeing each other. Whenever new members of staff joined the team, they treated Deb as their superior. She had the final say on most Wardrobe decisions. Then Win came along.'

Suzie chimed in, chocolate sauce lining her lips. 'Deb is incredibly good at her job. The team was great with her at the helm.'

'Mmm,' Bella agreed, taking her first bite of chocolate cake. 'Exactly. Win started off just like the rest of us, at bottom of the ladder. She was a fashion graduate when she came on board, with big dreams and high hopes.

'Around this time, Carl called things off with Deb, claiming that he wanted to focus on his wife and family. Deb was devastated. She'd started the ball rolling to divorce her husband and was under the impression that Carl was going to do the same. I comforted her as best I could.' Bella looked upset.

She continued, 'Win and Deb started to clash over a lot of creative decisions. Normally, Deb would have the ultimate say, but Carl started getting involved a lot more, and Win would usually come out on top. Desperate to prove that she was the best person to lead the team, Deb would be the first in the office and the last to leave. During one late night, she heard noises coming from Carl's office. Noises that were like the ones she'd made in there just a few months previously!'

'What?! Win and Carl are an item?' I blurted.

'Not exactly.' Suzie's cheeks flushed. 'We'll get to that.

At this point, I started working for FBW. Deb and I hit it off from the moment we met, and she confided in me about her suspicions. She was heartbroken about the whole thing—in the middle of a divorce and hopelessly pining for Carl.

'Deb, Bella and I set a few traps. A few random knocks on Carl's office door, regular late nights, stakeouts in the car park to see who left with whom...it was like being in a spy movie!' Suzi giggled.

'The company was still growing,' said Bella, 'Carl wanted to promote someone to Head of Wardrobe. Both Win and Deb jumped at the chance. Win became unbearable and acted as if she already had the job. After weeks of interviews, presentations and meetings, Win was given the role. There's little wonder that she and Deb can never see eye to eye.'

'I can understand,' I said. 'Poor Deb. Working closely with Win every day must take its toll.'

'At one of the Christmas parties, a few years ago, it all came out,' Bella added. 'We'd all had a bit too much to drink and Win was pressing a few buttons. Deb confronted her about the whole situation and Win just laughed. She didn't deny it, but she didn't confirm it, either. She tried to air Deb's dirty laundry instead. Carl's wife was at the party; it got so awkward. Deb nearly ended up with the sack. It was only her incredible work that saved her skin. Now, we all just keep our heads down and let Win carry on. Surely, you've noticed. Any man in power, she's all over them.'

'Has the scandal blown over now?' I asked.

They both shook their heads. 'I don't think they'll ever get along while they're working in the same department,' sighed Bella.

We eventually finished our desserts and went our separate ways. I couldn't stop thinking about everything I'd learned. No wonder Deb was being the way she was. In her eyes, the exact same scenario was playing out. Since I'd got closer to Richie, I'd been handed more opportunities, I couldn't deny it. But I wasn't trying to sleep my way to the top. I felt like I had a genuine connection with Richie. How could I get that across to Deb?

Chapter Sixteen

The next morning, the same thing happened, and I found myself working alone at the office. 'I'll come over later to see where you're at.' Win's smile was as fake as her veneers.

'Okay, but I finished all that paperwork yesterday.' I tried my hardest to keep the irritation out of my voice.

'Don't worry, I added more this morning. Ciao, darling!'

Since when did Win call me 'darling'? It made her sound like an evil villain in a movie. I sighed heavily. *Time to see what she's left me.*

***

Don't tell me they've locked you away at the office again.

Bless him, Richie must've been waiting for me to arrive on set. I was hoping he'd text; that way I could ensure he had his phone to hand and no curious eyes would see my messages.

Yes, but I think I know why. They're trying to keep us apart.

What?!

Be careful, Deb knows about us. I'll explain more when I see you.

My hands were shaking as I typed the words. I didn't want to reveal too much over a text. My phone vibrated almost as soon as the message was delivered.

Okay. But I'm going to find a way to see you today. I need to see you. Everything's going to be alright, I promise.

His response made me smile. He really did care. Surely, he wouldn't *really* be able to come to the office—they were in the middle of shooting. What excuse could he give?

Just over an hour later, there was a knock at the door

that made me jump out of my skin. When I opened it, Richie stood before me, looking like the Cheshire Cat who'd got the cream. 'Sorry I made you jump.' He held a large wad of paper in his hands.

'I didn't think you'd be able to come.' My grin matched his.

'I said I would. Don't you trust me?'

'Richie, you're in the middle of shooting a TV drama and you're the star of the show! They're going to notice if you go missing.'

He waved the wad of paper in my face. 'What good is an actor without his script?'

I rolled my eyes at him.

'What? Accidents happen!' He winked. 'So, I'll need this photocopying, please.'

I took the script from him and noted that my churning stomach of the last twenty-four hours had disappeared...everything now seemed completely fine. So, what if Deb knows about us, it's not that big a deal.

It was the first chance I'd had to explain everything to him. 'Deb saw us together. The other night, in the castle car park.'

'The light that was left on in Wardrobe? That was her? Dammit.'

'I'm don't know who she's told, if anyone. But I went out with them last night and, long story short, Deb lost out on a huge promotion because Win was sleeping around with the people that mattered. She's assumed the same thing is happening again.'

Richie let out a small laugh. I shot him a sharp look. 'Sorry. It's just that...hearing this from the other side of the fence, it's rather amusing.'

'You knew?'

'About Win? Yes, of course. From day one. You saw yourself how she tried to cast her spell over me too.' Richie shook his head. 'Penny, I come across girls like Win everywhere. They're all over the industry. But I'm not interested. I told you, I didn't come here looking for love, if you can call what Win offers love.' He took hold of my hands. 'I mean it, your magnetic field must be pretty damn strong.' I felt my cheeks flush.

'Well, Deb thinks otherwise. She thinks I'm out for her job.'

'And are you? Are you using me, Miss James?' Richie gazed at me intently, and I felt paralysed under his gaze. My feelings for him made his question ridiculous, but how could I tell him that without scaring him away? I didn't even know what we currently were. A fling? An on-set romance? A secret affair? Deep down, I knew we'd become much more than that.

'Never,' I whispered, leaning up and giving him the softest of kisses. A kiss that said a thousand words.

When we pulled apart, I was surprised to see a hint of pink in Richie's cheeks. He coughed. 'So, about this photocopying.'

'Yes, okay.' I loaded the script into the photocopier whilst Richie mooched around the office and mindlessly leafed through paperwork.

'Honestly, Penny, don't worry about this. I've got it all under control. There's only like a week left of shooting. If they want to keep you locked away back here all that time, then more fool them.' He paused for a second. 'And I've been thinking. This has kind of solidified everything for me. Once shooting is over, I want to take you away with me. I want to fly you far, far away, where it's just us. What do you say?' He perched on the edge of Suzie's desk.

'I say Suzie is going to freak out when she learns you've been sitting on her desk.'

'Don't avoid my question.' He arched an eyebrow, and my heart skipped a beat. 'Come away with me. Let's jet off to somewhere as beautiful as you.' He pushed himself up from the desk and pulled me to him. I felt the warmth of his breath on my cheeks.

'Okay. I'd love to,' I whispered.

He traced his fingers down my sides until they rested

on my hips. He then gripped my waist and hoisted me onto the photocopier. His lips brushed against mine and his tongue requested entrance. Just as I was about to succumb, I heard the familiar sound of a key card being swiped and the accompanying beep.

'Penny, I didn't think it would take you this long to-' Win stopped dead in her tracks. Richie and I had sprung apart but a second too late. We'd been caught, right in the act.

'Oh, sorry, I didn't know I had to knock.' She smiled slyly. I don't like this at all. Instead of blowing her top, like I expected her to, she just sneered at us for what felt like a lifetime. The awkward silence was eventually broken by Richie's ringtone.

Richie cleared his throat. 'My cue to leave,' he said, his voice monotonous. He picked up the papers from the end of the photocopier. 'Thanks for this.' He lowered his voice slightly and spoke pointedly in my direction, 'Catch you later, yeah?'

I nodded, then he went. Win continued to stare me down. I could tell she was dying to say something. I refused to break our gaze as she began circling me, like a predator surrounding its prey.

'I'm glad I saw it with my own eyes,' she said. 'You just couldn't take my advice, could you? And now you're done for. I'm not like Deb. I'll keep your dirty little secret, but you'll have to make it worth my while.'

Clearly, Deb had told Win. *Well, if you can't beat them...*

'Take my money, but you won't get away with it for long. I don't fancy your chances when all this comes to light. And I mean *all* of it.' I tried to lace my words with as much menace as possible.

Win let out one of her shrill cackles. 'Oh, Penny, I don't want your pennies! Ha! No, no, I want your loyalty, darling. You've earned rather a good name for yourself around here, and I want you on my side. Understood?'

I stared at her, not completely sure I understood.

'I have enough enemies, which you're clearly aware of. What I want from you is an alliance. Imagine what we could achieve if we combined our forces. It'll be magical. And don't worry about Deb. I've been trying to get rid of her for years.'

'Your blackmail might have been your greatest weapon before now, but it's not going to work on me. I didn't come here for power.' She squinted at me. Clearly no one had ever said no to her before.

'So, what are you here for then? Richie Clarke? Darling, don't waste your time. He won't even remember your name in a week, trust me.'

I didn't even dignify her comment with a response and walked out of the office. Whatever Win's plan was, I wanted no part of it.

***

'I need to tell you something.'

Mum had been curious as to why I'd arrived home so early. The fact I'd offered to cook dinner was also frying her brain. She stared at me, doe eyed, mindlessly chewing the same mouthful.

'I'm kind of, sort of, seeing Richie Clarke... And it might have landed me in a boatload of trouble.'

The silence stretched on. Of all the ways this had played out in my head, I hadn't expected this. 'Mum, are you okay?'

'Sorry, dear, I was processing what you said.' There was another pause. 'Isn't Richie Clarke in his forties?'

I had to stifle a laugh. Of all the things Mum could have been concerned about, it was Richie's age. 'Yes, he's forty-two.'

'Going for older men now, are we?' She smiled. 'Well, you sure know how to pick them. He's a handsome devil.'

'We've been trying to keep it a secret, what with Richie's profile and his divorce and everything. But people have started to find out and, honestly, I'm terrified. It's not about my job or anything, I just don't want the paparazzi chasing me everywhere or my name dragged through the mud. You, Dad and Aunt Ange exposed. Richie's reputation in shreds.' I spoke without really thinking, it all gushed out of me. I already felt a weight lift from my shoulders. 'I wanted to ask your advice. What should I do?'

'You're a grown woman now. You're allowed to make your own choices.'

I bit my lip. Did that mean she didn't approve?

'What happens in your love life is none of my business. Learning that you're dating a celebrity is a bit of a shock, I won't lie. If it's what you both want, and I stress both, I think you should go for it. Who cares what other people think? It's your happiness, Penny.'

I got up from my chair to give her the tightest hug. 'I love you. And thank you. I can't wait for you to meet him.'

'I love you too, honey,' she whispered back.

Chapter Seventeen

Millie's fiancé, Zach, had booked us a private room at one of the dingiest karaoke bars I'd ever seen. When Richie had invited me along, I hadn't expected this. The floor was sticky, the air smelt of stale tobacco and the room would've been pitch black, if not for the tacky neon signs illuminating slogans such as *VIBES* and *GOOD TIMES*. It was the last place I would have ever imagined a bunch of actors hanging out. Maybe that was the idea.

Apparently, tensions had been running high on set and Millie suggested that everyone needed a break. I hadn't been on set in four days and, according to Millie, Richie had pined for me. Some of Richie's friends were also there; they were all aware of who I was, and no questions were asked. I found out that they were all actors too. Some had enjoyed lead roles and others worked as supporting cast. A few were extras. They all knew each other from 'back in the day'.

At 'Gary's Boogie Nights Bar' alcohol flowed like water. Richie had his arm around my shoulders, pulling me close. Dan, one of Richie's friends, was completely murdering My Way on the mic.

'Having a nice time?' Richie whispered. He was already slurring his words. *That hadn't taken very long.*

'Mmm.' I was a little worse for wear too. I looked up at Riche's face and my heart just swelled. He seemed so content. That's not to say he was always unhappy or stressed, it's just, tonight, he appeared completely at ease and happy with the world.

I put my hand on his leg. Not suggestively, or possessively, just contentedly. The alcohol made me feel more confident than usual. My hand slowly crept upwards and Richie's smile widened. His leg muscles were hard and defined. Quietly powerful...and sexy as hell.

'I think you should sing,' he muttered.

I nearly snorted my drink up my nose and Richie chuckled. 'What! Me? Hell, no! Especially not in a room full of people well acquainted with performing arts.'

'Acquainted with performing arts?' said Richie. 'You mean 'went to drama school instead of getting a real degree',' he winked.

'I'm going to politely decline your offer.'

To my dismay, drunk Richie wasn't prepared to take no for an answer. 'Penny! Penny! Penny!' he chanted, as Dan's tenth song finally finished. The whole gang joined in, banging the table and stamping their feet.

'Yes!' Millie squealed over them. She clapped her hands together enthusiastically. 'Go on, Penny, I'd love that!' Her eyes were wide and hopeful. How could I say no to that? I look around them all; I was the youngest there, but I was actually surrounded by a bunch of big kids.

'Fine.' I got to my feet and gave a mock sigh while everyone cheered. 'Hang on, hang on! I'll need another drink first. Someone can fill in for me while I grab another bottle.' Millie had to hold Dan back–he was more than ready to go up again. I wobbled slightly on the way to the bar and was steadied by Richie who wrapped his arm around my waist.

'Careful,' he teased. 'You know, I was only joking in there.' He propped himself up on the bar. Still slurring, he said, 'You don't have to sing.'

I played with the hair at the nape of his neck. 'I know. But I will. I have a song that I think everyone will appreciate.'

'I'm intrigued.' He kissed my palm affectionately. It was so liberating to be out with him like this, without the fear of someone spying on us.

Back in the private room, drink in hand, my song choice was easy to find. As the intro played, I took one last gulp of wine before picking up the microphone. I soon lost myself in the music.

'I want to break free. I want to break freeeeeee!' It was just like singing in the shower. 'I want to break free from your lies, you're so self-satisfied. I don't need you. I've got to break free.
God knows, God knows I want to break free.'

I could vaguely hear cheers of approval from my audience. The lyrics rolled off my tongue and I breathed more and more life into the words as I went on. Queen's lyrical genius had always spoken to me, but now I was living it, breathing it. I embodied it.

'I've fallen in love. I've fallen in love for the first time and this time I know it's for reaaaal. I've fallen in love, yeah. God knows, God knows I've fallen in love. I want, I want, I want, I want to break freeeeee!'

The final bars of the song played out and I broke out of my trance. Everyone around the table clapped and whistled. As I returned to my seat, I felt a couple of pats on my back and my wine glass had magically been refilled.

'Well done, baby.' Richie pulled me into an embrace. He nuzzled his nose into my neck and planted the lightest of kisses.

'Hey, Richie, when is it your turn? Dan tugged on Richie's sleeve.

'Oh no, you won't catch me up there. Especially after that performance.' Richie raised his glass in my direction.

'That's not fair! Especially after you forced poor Penny up there,' Millie chimed in.

'Was I so wrong to do so?' Richie tried to deflect Dan's request. 'She was incredible!'

'Richie! Richie! Richie!' Zach began chanting, and everyone quickly joined in. Just as Richie was about to crack, the door swung open to reveal an irritated blonde man in a hot pink 'Gary's Boogie Nights Bar' polo shirt.

'Sorry, guys, we close in five.'

There was a chorus of groans.

'Saved by the bell,' I said to Richie as we all scrambled to collect our things. He simply grinned and draped my coat around my shoulders.

Once outside in the crisp evening air, the alcohol really hit me. I felt as though my knees were about to buckle. I saw Dan and Stuart arm in arm, signing one final rendition of *My Way*, and Zach and Millie cosying up together. Richie put his arm around my waist protectively and practically carried me down the road. It was a truly lovely moment, and one I would treasure for a long time.

'Thanks.' I rested my head on his shoulder, savouring the last few moments of the evening before we returned to reality. 'It's been a fantastic evening, exactly what the doctor ordered. Now for the taxi.'

'What taxi?' Richie laughed.

'My taxi home.' His laughter was apparently infectious as I began laughing too. 'I live, like, an hour away. I can't crawl there.'

'Don't be silly. You're staying with me.'

'Sorry?'

'I said...you're staying with me.' He scooped me up into a fireman's lift, catching me completely off guard. I shrieked way too loudly for that time on a Thursday night.

'Like I was going to let you go home alone after having that much to drink.' Richie was completely unperturbed by my squeals. 'What do you take me for?'

I was too busy giggling to answer. I had no idea what was going on anymore, but I was enjoying myself immensely. I don't think I'd ever acted so impulsively in my entire life.

'Goodnight, guys,' Richie shouted to the others before jogging ahead with me still slung over his shoulder.

'Careful, you'll drop her!' I heard Millie's concern somewhere in the distance. By the time I managed to lift my head we'd already rounded a corner and they were gone.

Despite our condition, we made it to Richie's hotel in one piece. He'd eventually put me down and we'd stumbled together, holding hands, and swinging them around in an exaggerated manner. We didn't stop laughing the entire journey.

In the lift, we couldn't keep our hands off each other. His lips were on mine, then they were down my neck and across my collarbone. My hands were in his hair then under his shirt, then cradling his right buttock. *Maybe I've died and gone to heaven.* He fumbled around for his key card, and we practically fell into the hotel room and onto the bed without breaking contact.

'I'm just going to freshen up,' I said, finally breaking away from him. He nodded and released me from his grip. Scampering into the bathroom, I carefully shut the door behind me. In the mirror I could see a grin on my face that stretched from ear to ear. Despite all the drama around us, tonight had left me feeling so very free. And it seemed as if the night wasn't ready to end quite yet.

I giddily stripped off my clothes, which wasn't easy, thanks to my inebriated state. I eventually managed it and was confronted by the reflection of my nearly naked self.

Why didn't I put on nicer underwear? I scowled at the mirror. *It's too late to worry about it now.* I reached for Richie's toothbrush and quickly started scrubbing at my teeth and tongue. I didn't want to keep him waiting.

I opened the door and summoned my inner goddess of seduction. I was appalled to see Richie on the bed with his eyes closed. On cue, I heard him snore loudly. It was a real slap in the face.

'Really, Richie?' I sighed. I got under the sheets on the other side of the bed. I reasoned that we'd both had a lot to drink; I lost count a long while ago. Maybe it was for the best.

I must have disturbed him getting into bed because I

felt his arms snake around me and feather-light kisses peppering my neck. I wasn't as in the mood as I had been a moment ago, especially because I knew there was a very real chance he might fall asleep in the middle of any lovemaking. And how mortifying would that be?! Plus, I was wearing the worst pair of knickers I owned.

'It's okay,' I whispered. 'Baby steps.'

'Baby steps,' he murmured in agreement. Snuggled together, we were silent for a few minutes. I began to think he'd dropped back off to sleep until I heard him sing softly amid the darkness.

'On a dark desert highway, cool wind in my hair.
Warm smell of colitas, rising up through the air.
Up ahead in the distance, I saw a shimmering light.
My head grew heavy, and my sight grew dim.
I had to stop for the night.'

I closed my eyes and just listened to the sound of his voice. After the first chorus, his rendition petered out.

'Was that going to be your karaoke song?' I asked, sleepily.

I felt him nod beside me.

I drifted to sleep in his arms. Maybe tonight wasn't the night I was going to sleep with the Richie Clarke. But I was more than happy with how it ended.

***

Getting up for work the next morning was a definite struggle. Especially given I'd woken up in Richie Clarke's arms. But we eventually managed it, after many grunts and groans. At first, Richie was a little sheepish around me and apologetic about his actions the previous evening. But I'd had the best night of my life; I wasn't complaining.

Continuing to be brave and bold, Richie held my hand as we left the hotel. With a heavy heart, I remembered that I might not be welcome on set. After agonising over whether to just turn up unannounced, I decided to phone Win for the state of play.

'I'm afraid I need you at the office today, Penny. I've

got something important for you,' she said in a sickly-sweet tone. My shoulders slumped.

Richie tried his best to cheer me up, even going out of his way to drop me at the office.

'Text me as soon as you know what this 'important thing' is.' I could see in Richie's eyes that he didn't want to go without me.

'Even if it's something daft, like another pile of paperwork?'

'Yes.' He leaned over to steal a quick kiss. 'Have a good day. I'll speak to you later.'

The building was eerily quiet. I knew I wasn't the only person there, but on the way up to Wardrobe, I didn't come across a single person. Opening the office door, I expected another gigantic pile of paperwork waiting for me; however, Win's desk had been cleared. The only thing on it was a small white envelope addressed to Miss. P. James. I sat down and tore it open.

Dear Miss James,

With deepest regret, your contract with FBW Productions is being terminated. As stated in said contract, your legal statutory notice is one week. However, due to the nature of the business, we require that your notice be served at the main FBW Productions' office. You will not be required at any of the company's mobile locations.

We would like to thank you for your contributions during your time at FBW Productions and we wish you all the best with any future endeavours.

Yours sincerely,
Carl Wright
CEO, FBW Productions

I stared at the letter in horror. Deep down, this wasn't a surprise—I'd guessed this was coming but I'd tried to convince myself otherwise. Win was a powerful woman and not someone you wanted to get on the wrong side of—the proof of that was in my hands.

Eventually, I folded the letter and placed it back into the envelope with a heavy sigh. Last night, I'd been on top of the world, now I felt worthless and hollow. I relayed the information to Richie via text, as promised.

Hi Richie, I'm not really sure how else to put this, but they've given me my notice.

Once the message had been sent on its way I sat back and fully reflected on the letter. Was it so bad? Richie, Millie, Dan, Stuart—my real friends there—would all be leaving FBW once filming was complete. I'd miss Suzie and Bella, of course, but I could still meet up with them outside work. It helped to put everything in perspective; that being said, I couldn't stop the feelings of emptiness.

I knew Richie would be in Make-up, so I didn't expect him to reply for a few hours. I was surprised to see an incoming call from his phone a few minutes later.

'Tell me this isn't because of us.' There was a coolness to his voice.

I couldn't honestly say. 'I don't know. My job was never guaranteed, I suppose. But everything was going so well before, I thought there may have been a chance...' I left the sentence hanging in the air.

Even if that chance *had* been clouded by my interaction with Richie Clarke, I wouldn't have changed it.

'Do you want me to have a word, see what I can do?'

I thought about it. *Do I want Richie to intervene? Do I want to work with corrupt, power-hungry people like Win, Deb, Carl, and God knows who else? Do I want to be in any role that only exists because Richie Clarke insisted on it? Do I want to be a glorified coffee runner that badly?*

'I appreciate the offer, Richie, I really do. But it's okay. I want to break free, remember?' I hoped he'd get the reference. 'This has just helped me with a decision I was destined to make, that's all.'

'So, what will you do now? Simply leave? I'm tied in my contract until filming ends, unfortunately. I won't be able to take a stand with you. My agent would kill me, he really would.'

'Don't be daft, I'd never ask that of you.' His loyalty brought a lump to my throat. 'Besides, my contract doesn't officially finish until filming has wrapped. I've just got to spend the next week alone, in the office. Don't worry, I'll make the most of it.' Unintentionally, I let out a deep sigh.

'Okay,' he said quietly, then the line went dead.

Chapter Eighteen

Richie must've managed to twist someone's arm, because the next day I was invited back on set. However, I was Riche's P.A. more than anything else. I had a make-shift desk in his trailer, and I accompanied him to all his shoots as his personal dresser. It was my dream job, even if it was only going to last a few days, until filming finished.

'Penny!' Suzie rushed over as Richie and I left his trailer one morning. 'Sorry to hear the bad news. I was gutted when they told me.'

I met her gaze, searching for signs of insincerity. I loved Suzie and her goofiness, but I wasn't sure who I could trust anymore. She looked like she could burst into tears any second and seemed quite genuine.

I gave her a small smile. 'Thanks, Suzie.'

She enveloped me in a warm hug. 'Honestly, Penny, you've been fabulous. I thought you'd be here for the long haul. I don't know what they're thinking.'

'Oh, don't worry about it.' I tried to dismiss her sympathy with a wave of my hand, but a lump stuck in my throat.

It had taken me a while to come to terms with the termination of my contract. I eventually concluded that it was the best thing for me, for the company, and, more importantly, for mine and Richie's future (should there be such a thing).

'You'll be missed,' said Suzie, a single tear running down her cheek. I reached over to hug her again, but she waved me away. 'Don't worry about me. I'm just being silly.' She rubbed her eyes and smeared her mascara in the process. Richie offered her a tissue from his pocket and Suzie's face turned crimson. *Poor thing.* I heard her take a deep breath to steady herself. 'I wanted to ask if you were still going to the Halloween wrap party.'

'Wrap party?' This was the first I'd heard of it. I looked from Suzie to Richie then back to Suzie again.

'At the castle on Friday night,' she said. 'Has no one invited you?' Suzie threw Richie a pointed look.

'Well, consider this your invite. Friday night. Eight o'clock. At the castle. Because it's Halloween, fancy dress is encouraged, but it's optional...though I think most people will be up for it. See you there, I hope.'

I nodded, the cogs in my brain turning. She waved her goodbyes and scampered away.

I waited until she'd gone then turned to Richie. 'Why didn't you tell me about the wrap party?'

Richie ran his fingers through his hair. 'I didn't think you'd want to go...' He paused. '...given the circumstances.'

I let out a loud laugh. 'Oh no, Richie, I wouldn't miss it for the world.'

***

'I'll take you, then you can have a drink.' Mum's voice was chirpy.

'Okay, fine. But Mum, you have to promise not to do anything...embarrassing.'

Mum wrinkled her nose. 'What do you mean embarrassing?'

'I don't know...' I could hear Aunt Ange laughing quietly. 'Something like...always carrying my baby pictures in your purse and showing complete strangers.'

'But you were such a cute baby,' Mum protested.

'And lying about your age every day since the age of twenty-nine.' Aunt Ange joined in.

'Ange!' Mum looked at her in horror. 'Call yourself my sister!'

'Playing your music really loud in the car, especially the Mamma Mia soundtrack.' I added. 'Getting people's attention from a distance by shouting *Cooee!* Asking for assistance from the one person in the shop who wears all black but doesn't actually work there.'

'Telling the cute guy at the coffee shop, when Penny was a baby, that she was your niece,' muttered Aunt Ange.

'Mother!' I gasped.

'Okay, okay. I promise I won't say or do anything that will embarrass you at the party. There.'

Aunt Ange patted my hand. 'I'll take you, Pen. Eight o'clock, did you say?'

I grinned. 'Fabulous, it's a date!'

'Wait a minute-' Mum started to object.

'Sorry, Mum. I'm afraid I can't risk it. Love you!' I scurried off to get ready.

***

'If you need a lift back, don't hesitate to call me. And if you don't, well, be sure to text your Mum so she knows you're safe.'

I rolled my eyes. 'Aunt Ange!' I leaned over and kissed her cheek. 'Thanks for the lift.' I got out of the car and started down the slope towards the castle entrance. Aunt Ange's horn beeped. 'Don't do anything I wouldn't do!' she shouted.

'Don't worry, I won't!'

Though I'd only had two days' notice, I was quite with pleased with my costume. I was a black cat, sultry and sexy—for Richie's benefit, of course. I'd dug out one of my favourite black jumpsuits and paired it with a black ribbon choker, to which I'd attached a little bell. I'd bought a cat ear headband and fashioned a tail out of some black crushed velvet and faux fur oddments from my fabric stash. I'd made my eyes look like a cat's and drawn on a cute set of whiskers with eyeliner. In my black kitten heels, the path felt like a runaway.

I'd got Aunt Ange to drop me off half an hour after the party had started, in an attempt to be fashionably late. I was pleased to find my two favourite Wardrobe girls hanging out by the entrance. 'Hey, ladies!'

'Love the outfit, Penny,' Bella exclaimed, taking my

hand and twirling me around. I made sure to wiggle my bum, to show off my perfectly crafted cat's tail. Bella sported an elaborate witch's gown and Suzie wore a black unitard with an impressive skeleton attached to the front and back. *These ladies are so talented.*

'Isn't that Richie?' Suzie nudged my arm. I looked in the direction of where she was pointing and there he was: *Richie Clarke—Vampire.*

'Maybe I can get him to buy us a drink.' I smiled mischievously at Suzie. 'Come on.'

'You coming?' Suzie asked Bella.

'Actually, I'd better see what Deb's up to,' she said. 'You two go. Enjoy yourselves, it's wrap night!'

Suzie and I approached Richie, who was talking to Millie and Zach, as well as a few other members of the cast and crew that I didn't recognise. I'd imagined that our relationship was public knowledge by now, but apparently, not everyone knew.

'Hey, Richie, how's it going?' I strived to keep my voice light and simply amicable, so that those who didn't know we were a couple wouldn't suspect anything (which was difficult, as Richie was pulling off that vampire look). No one reacted or appeared to even notice.

'Good evening, ladies!' As an actor, he was much better at pretending than I was. 'Having a nice night?' he said in a mock-Transylvanian accent. His false fangs gave him a tiny lisp, which I found utterly adorable.

'Yes, thanks. You?'

'Fine. Fffhank you,' he replied.

'We were wondering if you fancied buying two of your biggest fans a drink.' I said, as innocently as I could.

He grinned, his fangs on show. 'How could I say no?' Richie excused himself from the group and followed us.

At the bar, Richie extended a glass of wine towards Suzie. 'This is for you. Thank you for helping me look so fabulous these last few weeks.'

'T-thank you,' she stammered. 'Really, the pleasure's

all mine.'

I suppressed a smile. Suzie had been such a good friend to me. Ensuring that Richie expressed his gratitude was the least I could do.

'To my biggest fans. Cheers!' He raised his glass and we both followed suit. As planned, Richie kissed me on both cheeks then did the same to Suzie. She could hardly contain herself.

Richie and I passed polite conversation until Suzie had recovered enough to talk. It just took a few big gulps of wine. 'I better go check on Bella,' she said eventually.

'Yeah, sure.' I smiled.

'Thank you again, Richie. It was very nice of you.' Suzie raised her glass to him. 'Have a lovely evening.' With that, she disappeared into the crowd.

'Did I do okay?' asked Richie.

'Nailed it.'

'Teamwork makes the dream work,' he chuckled.

'You're such a goofball, you know that?'

'Takes one to know one.'

When we'd finished our drinks, he led me to the dancefloor, where we swayed to a couple of songs. It wasn't crowded, but I still ensured there was no physical gap between us.

'I like your outfit,' he said.

'Thanks. I made the tail myself.'

'This I have to see.' He twirled me around. 'Very nice.'

'I could say the same about you,' I purred into his ear. 'Did I ever tell you that Twilight was one of my favourite books when I was a teen?'

I felt him laugh. 'I aim to please.'

Suddenly, I heard a familiar beat.

'Dun, dun, dun... Another one bites the dust.'

'They're playing my request!' Richie's eyes twinkled. 'It is *Queen* you like, isn't it?'

The glee on my face gave him the answer. He lowered me backwards over arm and brought his lips close to my neck.

'Mind if I take a bite?' His fangs glinted in the disco lights.

'Please do.' I said breathily, my body yearning for his. But just when I thought he was going to make contact, he brought me back up.

'Not now, kitty. Maybe later.' He grinned when he saw my pout. We continued with our private tango until the song finished. 'I think I owe you another drink.' He took my hand and led me back to the bar where the bartender presented us with two wine glasses.

'Cheers,' he raised his glass to mine for the second time that evening.

'Cheers,' I echoed.

'To happy endings and new beginnings.'

I gave him the smallest peck on the cheek. I knew I wouldn't be able to resist him for the whole night.

'A cat. How imaginative.' Win flipped the hair of her 'Zombie Cleopatra' wig. I took a deep breath. I'd managed to avoid her since our last, rather heated, conversation.

'Look, Win, just enjoy your night and let me enjoy mine. In fact, let me buy you a drink.'

'Don't try and take the high ground with me, Penny James,' she scoffed. She was obviously drunk; she was swaying on the spot and sloshing her glass of red wine. She raised her voice to be heard above the music. 'You're nothing, darling. If it wasn't for me, you wouldn't even be here. And you certainly wouldn't be smooching Richie Clarke.' As soon as the words left her lips, it was as if the party stopped.

'Whoops!' Win covered her mouth in mock shock, but even that couldn't hide the grin spreading across her face.

'At least I'm only interested in men who are *available*, unlike some people,' I retorted. Win's vicious smile began to fade. 'I know everything. How you walked all over Deb, how you sleep your way into everyone's good books. How you're just bitter and jealous because you didn't manage to sink your claws into Richie.'

'Come away, Win.' Carl suddenly appeared. He was unable to look Richie or me in the eye. He took Win by the arm and tried to lead her away, but she resisted.

'Go ahead,' I continued, 'tell the world I'm nothing. Tomorrow I'm leaving with this gorgeous man, and you'll still be here, chasing after other people's husbands.'

Win snarled like a rabid dog. 'You're messing with the wrong bitch! I will end you, Penny James,' she hissed.

'Goodbye, Win,' I replied calmly.

'Ciao!' she yelled, as Carl succeeded in dragging her away.

The room was silent. You could've heard a pin drop.

'Nicely handled,' Richie whispered. 'Do you want me to do anything? I could probably get her fired if I threatened to pull my parts from the show.'

'Thank you, Richie, but that won't be necessary.' I watched Win retreat until the crowd consumed her. 'In this business, I'd imagine there's always at least one diva. Besides, after tomorrow, she'll be out of my hair forever.'

Richie moved to kiss me but stopped when he realised how many eyes were still upon us.

'Well, the cat's out of the bag now.' I couldn't resist touching my cat ears to accentuate my point. We both giggled and Richie closed the gap between us. He gently kissed me in front of everyone from FBW Productions. It felt fantastic.

After we broke apart, I looked around. Although the party had resumed, it was obvious that people were staring at us. I suddenly felt uncomfortable.

'Shall we?' Richie offered me his arm, which I accepted gratefully. 'This party is a little dead anyway.' He nodded towards a couple dressed as zombie corpses.

I gave his arm a playful shove. 'My pun was better.' I felt relief wash over me as we made our exit.

Chapter Nineteen

Soon, we were in Richie's hotel room, with our lips locked and our eyes closed. Now our romance was exposed, and the weight of the secret had left my shoulders, I felt a new bout of confidence.

Richie nuzzled his face into my neck, which sent shivers down my spine and made my toes curl with pleasure.

'Richie,' I breathed. He took the strap of my jumpsuit between his teeth and pulled it over my shoulder. He twirled me round so I faced the wall and continued trailing kisses down my back. He then pulled the rest of the fabric away in one short, sharp movement.

My jumpsuit slid to the floor, and I was left standing in my skimpy black thong. *Thank God I decided against Spanx.*

'Meow,' Richie purred, guiding me towards the bed. I could feel the heat rising in my cheeks; I wasn't normally one to get embarrassed, but I'd also never stood in an itty-bitty thong in front of Richie Clarke. My embarrassment quickly subsided and was replaced with the overwhelming urge to kiss him. Fuelled by passion, our teeth clashed for dominance and our tongues swirled. We rolled around the bed. My hands were in his hair, twisting and tugging. One of his hands gripped my shoulder blade whilst the other cupped my left buttock.

'You're wearing too many clothes,' I panted. I broke apart from our kiss just long enough to push the hair out of my face.

'I do apologise.' He grinned and unbuttoned his jeans, throwing them on the floor. 'I'm afraid my underwear is nowhere near as exciting as yours.'

I looked down at his tight black boxers, my gaze lingering longer than intended. My hands traced the muscular definition of his chest, then trailed down to his stomach. 'Hmm, I'm afraid we'll have to agree to disagree on that one.'

Richie moaned. He wrapped his arm around me and flipped us over, so that he was on top. 'I can lose more clothes, but only if you keep those cat ears on,' he whispered in my ear, before tracing delicate kisses down my neck once more.

I woke the next morning feeling like a new woman. The whole world felt softer, calmer somehow. I glanced at the sleeping beauty next me, and it was almost enough for me to believe I'd died and gone to heaven. Relaxed in slumber, I could fully take in the beauty of Richie's features: his strong jawline; his Cupid's bow; those immaculate eyelashes that many men seemed to inherit which women could only dream of; the smattering of freckles across his cheeks and the bridge of his nose. Last night had been an absolute dream.

I supposed everyone had to wake up at some point. My phone screen said it was seven-thirty a.m. *Time to get up and face the day.* I quietly snuck out of bed and went into the bathroom to call a taxi. I gave the destination as the FBW office; I needed to collect my things now my contract had officially ended.

I wasn't sure what would happen next for Richie and me. I was hoping we'd talk about it last night, but in the end, we didn't do much talking. I debated whether to wake him and let him know I was leaving, so that we could arrange when and where to see each other next.

The voice of my self-doubt came in my head, nagging me to leave him be. It was afraid that, if I woke him, I'd have to confront the things I didn't want to hear. So, I left him sleeping.

I'd never had a one-night stand before and, to be honest, I'd never really wanted to. I'd heard so many stories before I even started at FBW Productions—the celebrity scandals, on-set flings, how some climbed the career ladder by going to bed with the important people.

From Rags to Richie

It didn't feel like that with Richie and me. Last night happened because we'd both wanted it to. He'd stuck by me again and again during the production, even after we'd been exposed. He'd had multiple opportunities to throw in the towel, to let me go—yet here he still was.

That was all well and good, but the world of celebrity culture was not one I inhabited. I wasn't aware of the etiquette; I didn't know what was going to happen next. I just hoped it wouldn't be goodbye. I kissed his beautifully soft lips before I left and made sure it was the sweetest kiss I'd ever given.

***

Struggling with the door of the FBW offices, I heard the toot of a car horn behind me. Presuming it to be Win ready for Round 2, I pretended not to hear. I then heard a car door slam and footsteps approaching.

'Need a hand?' I looked up to see Richie in a checked shirt, jeans, and some very large, dark sunglasses. Gratefully, I accepted his help, and we went to collect my things.

'Are you hungover?' I asked, once we were back at his car.

'Of course.' He grinned. 'Brunch?'

'I'd love that.'

'Well, buckle up then, babe. We're out of here. Toodles.' He waved to the office building. His car purred to life, the radio blaring out the legendary Freddie Mercury and The Show Must Go On.

'Great music choice.'

'Thanks. I thought it rather appropriate. Ready?'

'Definitely.'

Richie's grin was infectious.

It gave me comfort to imagine Win watching from one of the office windows. If she was, she'd have seen me being whisked away in Richie's Mercedes, the roof down, music blaring, and our matching Cheshire Cat smiles on display for the whole world to see.

***

'You need to stop running away from me. I'm not going anywhere.'

Richie had taken us to the cutest café I'd ever seen. It was like he knew every hidden gem in the world. It was the perfect blend of beauty and seclusion, all stained oak with peacock blue and brass trimmings. The menu offered luminous green matcha lattes and sourdough toast with baked beans, which came in a miniature saucepan. Richie ordered Eggs Benedict. I'm surprised he could stomach it with his hangover, but he tucked in enthusiastically when the dish was served. I couldn't blame him—the food was delicious.

'Let me take you away,' he said. I nearly choked. 'I meant what I said before. Let's go somewhere, just the two of us. I want to get to know you, Penny. Properly.' His eyes sparkled.

I didn't know what to say after enduring thoughts of never seeing him again. *Surely, he couldn't get to know me any more intimately than he did last night...*

'Umm...' My mouthful of food gave me a few more seconds to think about my reply. I looked into his beautiful blue eyes and realised I was being ludicrous. Richie Clarke, the famous actor, was asking to whisk me away, after we'd shared a phenomenal night together. I was twenty-seven, single and currently unemployed. *What is there to mull over?! What the hell have I got to lose?*

'I don't know what to say. Thank you? Yes, please?' I could feel excitement bubbling up inside.

'I hope you have a passport.'

My eyes widened. 'What! Why? Where are we going?'

'You'll see.' Richie winked then continued to polish off his Eggs Benedict. I badgered him for answers, but he refused to tell me more. *My FBW chapter may be over, but my journey with Richie Clarke has only just begun.*

Chapter Twenty

When I arrived at the airport a week later, I was still in the dark. All Richie had said was to pack for a beach holiday. I pulled along a suitcase full of bikinis and maxi dresses, hoping to God he wasn't playing a joke on me.

We'd agree to meet there, at the airport, but there was no sign of him. I waited for quite a while, my brain in overdrive. I chided myself for actually believing that Richie Clarke would still be interested in me once filming was done. *He probably only asked me on holiday because he felt sorry for me. He probably felt partially responsible for me being fired.*

I sighed and started walking towards the exit. A guy in a black beanie and dark shades touched my arm, making me jump out of my skin. It was only when he smiled that I recognised him. *I'd know that smile anywhere.*

Richie lifted his sunglasses. 'Sorry to make you jump. Public spaces and all that.' He glanced over his shoulder. 'Ready?'

I nodded, suddenly uneasy about the bustling airport.

'Fab, let's go,' he whispered. I reached for his hand, but he moved it away. My eyes snapped up to his face. 'Sorry.' He seemed nervous. 'Just in case. I promise, once we're on the plane, I'm all yours.' The sunglasses covered a good portion of his face, and I couldn't quite gauge his reaction.

Why did I not expect this? I suppose I'd taken the luxury of a private set for granted. Outside, in the big wide world, Richie was hot gossip. Bella was always telling me that his every movement filled pages of her gossip mags. The steakhouse incident should've confirmed that for me. People would pay big bucks for a snap of Richie Clarke running away on holiday with a new girlfriend so soon after his divorce.

I took a deep breath and matched Richie's pace as we marched through airport security and towards our gate—luckily, without any interruptions. It wasn't until we were comfortably seated on the plane that I realised...I still didn't have a clue where we were going. I'd been so focused on us getting on board without drawing any attention to ourselves that I hadn't even looked at the airport screens, and Richie had our tickets.

After the safety announcements, and once we were finally in the air, I turned to Richie. 'So, are you going to tell me our destination?'

By now, he'd removed his hat and glasses; those dazzling eyes were mine to behold. He squeezed my hand. 'I'll tell you in a bit.'

'You're such a tease!'

'I do aim to please,' he whispered, reaching for his earphones.

'Oh, come on,' I groaned. 'You've got to tell me *something.*'

'Alright, alright. I'm taking you to my family's holiday home. It's where we all go to escape the everyday. I thought it would make the perfect break after everything that's happened.' He smiled wistfully.

An absurd thought occurred. 'Richie, are you taking me to meet your parents?'

He burst out laughing. 'God, do you really think I'd be that cruel? Getting to know you better by hanging out with my parents for a week?!' He was still chuckling. 'It'll just be the two of us, I'm afraid.'

Phew. 'Sounds perfect.' I grinned as Richie snaked his arm around my shoulders.

'If I were you, I'd try and get some sleep. We've got a couple of hours travelling ahead, and this isn't our only flight of the day. You may as well take advantage now.'

Richie occupied himself with the onboard

entertainment. I decided to take his advice and dozed off contently, snuggled against him.

***

'Come on!' Richie grabbed my hand as soon as we disembarked the plane. He led me out onto a quieter part of the airport runway. We turned a corner and were greeted by a sleek black helicopter. My jaw almost hit the floor. Surely this wasn't our next flight? We got closer and the pilot waved at us from the controls. I looked at Richie, aghast. He just grinned at me.

'The Clarke holiday home is a little more-' he tried to find the right word, '...isolated than the average property.'

I raised an eyebrow, but he didn't offer any more detail. We climbed into the helicopter. I was given a headset and shown how to buckle myself in. Then we were in the air again. I think part of me went into shock; all I could do was sit in silence.

'This view's breath-taking.' I heard Richie's voice through my headset. We flew over a turquoise ocean; it was the same colour as Richie's eyes. Waves crashed beneath us. Ripples reflected the morning sun and they glinted and sparkled as they danced around. It was mesmerising to watch.

'What about our bags?' I said into my microphone.

Richie turned his head from the view and took my hand. 'Don't worry. I've done this trip thousands of times. I know the airport drill by now. They'll most probably arrive a short while after we do. Penny, honestly, you've nothing to worry about.'

I vowed to stop asking questions and to simply enjoy the wonderful view. This was a holiday, after all—I was supposed be relaxing.

Eventually, we landed on an island that just minutes ago had been a mere speck in the distance. It was beautiful. Golden sand, crystal clear waves lapping the shore, and gigantic palm trees. It looked like a postcard.

Richie led me through the trees, and we reached a

clearing. Before us was a stunning two-storey villa.

'Wow,' I gasped.

'Wait until you see the inside.'

The villa was truly luxurious. The lounge was filled with cosy sofas and chairs, all pointing towards a huge television. There was a built-in music system, which Richie informed me was connected to speakers in almost every room. The open-plan kitchen had a beautiful view of the beach, and the ocean sparkled as far as the eye could see. The villa had five bedrooms, each with their own en-suite and balcony. At the other side of the villa was a games room, complete with a pool table, jukebox, table football and a shelf full of books and board games. Outside, the patio boasted a dining area, barbeque, pool, and hot tub, as well as access to its own private beach. *Paradise.*

Richie reminded me of a peacock as he gave me the guided tour of the magnificent villa, his virtual feathers out in full plume. I'd have been lying if I said I didn't enjoy it—it was an absolute dream. Something popped into my head as he showed me his world in all its glory...what had his ex-wife been thinking?

Richie suggested we went skinny-dipping in the ocean to recharge ourselves after the hours spent travelling. I took in the cheeky grin on his face and twinkle in in his eyes and agreed—it sounded the perfect way to wind down.

***

We spent the rest of that first day settling in. Richie took me round the rest of the island too; we arrived back just as our suitcases were being dropped off. As we unpacked, Richie told me tales of his childhood holidays at the villa—how he used to tease his sister by wearing a shark fin on his back when they were swimming in the sea. His father teaching him how to surf. How his mother would completely smother him in sun-cream because he burnt so easily. I loved it when he shared his stories. We were just a normal couple once you stripped back all the glitz and the glamour.

As the sun began to set, Richie led me onto the patio, where a candlelit dinner waited.

'How...?'

'I may have some helpers around here.' He grinned.

The food smelt delicious. 'What, like chefs?' I took a seat.

'Chefs, gardeners, security guards, cleaners. There's a whole team that lives here. Have done for years, they're practically family.'

'And you didn't think to tell me that we're not alone *before* we went skinny dipping?'

'Would you have still done it?'

'No, but-'

'Exactly. What a shame that would've been,' he said, and my cheeks flushed. 'I don't think they saw us, anyway. The whole idea is that we never see them, but they take care of everything. They're a team of ninja butlers.' He may have thought it amusing, but I shifted uncomfortably in my seat. I couldn't help but find it unsettling that, though we appeared to be alone on the island, there was a whole team of people living in cabins amongst the palm trees, who were there to attend our every need.

'With more than twenty state of the art security cameras, I can guarantee our safety.'

I wasn't convinced, nor any less embarrassed about stripping down to my birthday suit and frolicking about in the ocean. I also had the sensation of being watched. I finished my food as quickly as I could, suddenly eager to get back inside the villa. *I take it back, being with Richie Clarke is anything but normal.*

Chapter Twenty-One

The next day, I awoke to the sound of a speedboat arriving at our private beach. Richie was behind the wheel. It was sleek, sophisticated, and fast, like a bullet in the water.

'Glad you're awake,' he said when he came inside. 'Fancy a spin?' He nodded towards the boat and a life jacket that was waiting for me by the water's edge.

'You bet I do.'

I'd never been on a speedboat before. In fact, I'd never really been out to sea before, but I soon realised that I'd been missing a fantastic experience. Observing Richie at the wheel of the boat, I started to believe that there was no end to this man's talents. One minute we were cruising along, mesmerised by the sights, and the next, we were zipping across the waves at exhilarating speeds. It was a truly thrilling experience, and I didn't want it to end. I wished I could have forever preserved this moment, just me and Richie in the middle of the big, blue ocean.

He surprised me again the next day with a scuba-diving experience. After breakfast, he introduced me to Andre—a six-foot, bronzed beauty of a man, who handed us two wetsuits.

The water was warm and inviting. The seabed was a riot of colour, swarming with creatures of all different shapes and sizes. I was in awe of this tropical land and everything it had to offer—Richie included. It was breathtaking.

The following day, Richie arranged for the helicopter to fly us to the mainland, where we visited numerous cute boutiques and stylish independent stores. I was having the time of my life on this holiday already…spending the day eyeing up the latest fashion trends on another continent was just the cherry on top. No man had ever understood me this well: my wants, my needs, my likes, my dislikes. I was enjoying getting to know Richie better too, this happy-go-lucky, romantic guy, who just wanted to enjoy life. I also felt it would be easy to adapt to a jet-setting, glamorous lifestyle.

In contented silence, we walked down a cobbled side street, just soaking up the sun, sights, and delicious smells of the busy food market nearby. However, I was jolted from my reverie when a young woman approached us. She dropped her sunglasses to the bridge of her nose.

'Excuse me, sorry to bother you. But are you Richie Clarke?' Her question was delivered politely, in a British accent. She was a petite brunette with sun-kissed skin. Her long hair cascaded down her back in loose curls, which were pinned in place with a large, pink rose. My heart began to thud in my chest.

Richie was as cool as a cucumber. 'You got me,' he said, his palms raised in mock defence. 'And you are?'

'Clara. I'm a huge fan,' she gushed before quickly composing herself. 'I can't believe I bumped into you here of all places. Would you mind if I took a selfie? My friends will never believe I've met you.' She took her phone from her bag.

'Sure,' Richie replied. He removed his sunglasses and leant towards her for the photo.

'Thank you so much!' She beamed. 'Enjoy the rest of your day.' She turned on her heel in the direction she came, her focus on her phone screen.

I felt relief wash over me. I don't know why I was so panicked, it's not like Richie and I were a secret anymore. I just didn't like the idea of someone bursting our perfect little bubble.

'The Instagram generation, eh?' Richie said.

'That's my generation you're mocking,' I retorted, faking offence. Richie let out a snort of laughter, and I shoved him playfully.

He put an arm round my shoulders. 'I do apologise. Let me buy you a fancy cocktail to make up for it. Maybe you could even take a photo of it. Slap on a filter with the caption #*wishyouwerehere.*'

'Calm down, granddad,' I joked. I wrapped my arms around his waist and kissed him on the cheek. Our jibes continued until we reached the next bar.

Chapter Twenty-Two

A few fancy cocktails and a sarcastic Instagram post later, Richie suggested that we finished off our trip to the mainland with something good to eat. After a quick phone call, we had a reservation at one of his favourite restaurants.

'Our chariot awaits.' Richie led me outside into the warm evening air. Parked outside was a miniature red camper van perched on top of a scooter. The driver waved at us merrily.

'A Tuk-Tuk?' I tried to hide my shock. After the private helicopter and speedboat, I'd had high expectations.

'Of course.' He offered me his hand and helped me climb aboard. 'What better way to experience the sunset?'

I shouldn't have doubted him—the view on our way to the restaurant was spectacular. The sky burst into colour; swirls of orange, purple and pink reflected on the surface of the ocean. Everything glittered and twinkled in the dimming light. I felt the sea breeze on my cheeks and tropical air in my lungs…the Tuk-Tuk gave us a front row seat to Mother Nature's magnificence.

My hand rested on Richie's thigh, my nose was snuggled into the crook of his neck and my eyes were glued to the sunset. I felt cocooned in his love. If I had to choose one moment from our relationship to bottle and keep forever, it would have been that one.

Richie had talked highly of this restaurant on our journey here, and I wasn't disappointed. It was delightful. A blend of delicious native cuisine and modern interior design. Orb-shaped lanterns hung above us as we sat in glossy black booths, which gave us some privacy. There were so many variations of spicy noodle dishes, I began salivating just reading the menu.

'Are you having a good time?' Richie asked, between

our starter and main course.

'Absolutely. This place is gorgeous. The food's delicious!'

'I meant the holiday in general. But I'm glad you like it here.'

'Oh, I see. In that case...' I put down my glass and looked him dead in the eye. 'I'm having the time of my life! This holiday is the stuff of dreams and I'm so glad I'm spending it with you. I don't think I know enough words to describe how I feel if I'm honest.'

He beamed. 'Not bored of me yet, then? The novelty hasn't worn off?'

I shook my head but didn't say a word. I couldn't believe he thought that was even possible.

'Good. I was just checking.' His fiddled with the corner of his napkin. 'Because...,' he cleared his throat, 'I'm getting rather attached to you, Penelope James.' He leaned across the table and kissed me.

We had kissed in public before—he'd made it quite clear, since leaving FBW, that he no longer wanted us to be a secret. But this was different. This was passionate, intense, especially for a crowded room. The butterflies in my stomach began to flutter.

The waiter arrived at our table; he gently coughed to get our attention and we pulled away. Richie reached for my hand and held it tightly as our food was served. Perhaps we should've been embarrassed, being caught mid-smooch, but we were just too wrapped up in each other to care.

After we'd had our mains—and with a throbbing tongue, garlic breath and sweat on my brow—I went to freshen up in the ladies'. As I passed the final row of booths, a guy at the table reached out to stop me, his fingers curling around my wrist.

'How do you know Richie Clarke?' he said. He was small and weedy, almost rat-like. He prompted me further by nodding towards our table, where Richie was checking the notifications on his phone.

From Rags to Richie

I felt panic wash over me for the second time that day. I tried to think of something to say. 'Oh, I see. No, sorry to disappoint you. That's my boyfriend, Mark. We actually get this a lot.' I freed my arm from his grip and forced a smile. 'I keep saying I'll have to Google this Richie fellow. Excuse me.' I barged into the bathroom without looking back. Once inside, I locked myself in a cubicle and pulled out my phone.

Just been stopped by a guy sitting on his own at the table near the toilets. He asked about you.

Richie replied within seconds.

When you're done, we'll leave.

When I returned to our table, Richie was already on his feet, the bill paid. 'Sorry about dessert,' he said.

'Don't worry about it. I'm sure you'll make it up to me.' I glanced over my shoulder. The guy was now engaged in a phone call, though his gaze was still trained on us both.

In the privacy of the helicopter, I quizzed Richie on the guy's identity. 'Not a clue,' he shrugged. 'But I didn't like his style.' He was busy tapping away on his phone, so I left it. Within a few minutes, he let out an exasperated sigh. He showed me his phone screen, which displayed the selfie that girl had taken at the food market earlier that day. It had been edited within an inch of its life, of course; in the background, out of focus but still recognisable, was me. I hadn't even realised I was in the shot. In the caption, the girl had tagged the location.

'What happens now?'

Richie squeezed my hand. 'Nothing. The security on the island is incredibly robust. As long as you're okay with laying low in paradise?'

'I can't imagine anything worse,' I said, winking at him.

***

Luckily, our 'friend' from the restaurant appeared to have stayed quiet and the next day was drama-free. Richie suggested we spent our evening at the villa, in the hot tub with a bottle of champagne, under the stars. I jumped at the chance. I'd been dying to get in the hot tub since I'd laid eyes on it; being joined by Richie was just a bonus.

Richie let out a wolf-whistle as I lowered myself into the rippling water. My cheeks flushed bright red. I was only wearing a simple black bikini, nothing adventurous, but with just one look, Richie made me feel like a million dollars.

After lounging in the tub, sipping champagne, and talking idly about anything and everything for half an hour, Richie waded over and gave me a long, lingering kiss. We broke apart and I had to cover my mouth with my hand to hide my laughter. My bright red lipstick had smeared all over his face. I pointed to his reflection in the patio window and a grin spread across his lips.

'Bad girl,' he teased, washing his face in the water.

'I'm not a bad girl,' I countered. 'I just do bad things with you.'

'Is that right?' He raised an eyebrow. 'Care to show me an example?'

'Gladly, Mr Clarke.' I sat in his lap, the hot tub bubbling around us. We kissed again, but this time it was even more passionate. Our slippery hands roamed all over each other. Suddenly, I heard a rustling in the foliage around us. We stopped kissing and our eyes flew open.

'What was that?' I peered into the darkness. The rustling had stopped, but I was still on edge. 'Are there dangerous animals on this island?'

'Come on.' Richie was calm. He got out of the tub and offered me his hand. 'Let's take this inside.'

I stepped out of the tub and followed him indoors. Despite Richie's boasts about the island's security, I couldn't shake the feeling we were being watched.

Chapter Twenty-Three

On our sixth day we simply opted to laze on the private beach. I didn't need flashy boat rides and scuba-diving lessons to keep me entertained. I was just as content to lay on a sun lounger and devour the romance novel I'd picked up at the airport. Richie was in the sea. I'd occasionally spot him bobbing up and down as he swam past, and he'd give me the occasional goofy wave.

The whole scene was a slice of heaven. The sound of the ocean lapping against the sand relaxed me to the point of sleep. I was roused from my snooze when Richie came out of the sea. His wet body glistened, and I laid back again to gaze at him.

There it is again, the feeling of being watched.

I lifted myself onto my elbows and scanned the horizon. If I squinted, I thought I could make out the outline of a small boat out to sea, with what looked to be four or five people aboard.

'I thought we weren't supposed to see the service team?' I said, pointing at the boat.

Richie's face dropped. 'Shit!' He scooped up the rest of his clothes. 'Indoors. Now.'

I didn't argue, just grabbed all my things and followed him inside. Richie set about locking the doors and closing the blinds, despite it only being midday.

'What's wrong?' I asked as my heart thudded in my chest. He beckoned me to sit with him at the dining table.

'I think you knew that being with me would not be easy.' I nodded, my eyes wide. 'Well, this is one of those testing moments. I suppose we can't have the good without some of the bad.' He bit his lip. 'It's the press. They know we're here. My assistant has kept me updated; apparently, we're big news back home, Pen.

After that selfie went live, we've been featured in every celebrity gossip column. I didn't want to worry you…I thought we'd be safe here until it all blew over.'

I could see the hurt in Richie's eyes, that he felt he'd let me down. 'They're after the picture that will earn them the big money. They'll do whatever it takes to get it,' he added, his voice sombre.

'Surely all they want is a few photographs. With camera lenses these days, they should be able to get their shots without too much intrusion, shouldn't they? Then we can enjoy the rest of our holiday.'

Richie shook his head. 'I wish it were that simple.' He rubbed his thumb across my knuckles soothingly. 'I just wish we'd had a bit more time. It was the one part of my world I hoped wouldn't catch up with us. All I can do is apologise. We could probably board the helicopter without too much trouble if we leave tonight.'

'You're prepared to cut short our time here because of some guys with cameras in a rubber dingy? For all we know they could be extreme perverts.'

Richie managed a smile. 'So, you want to stay then?'

'I do.' I leaned over to kiss him gently. 'I'm getting rather attached too.'

Richie was grinning now. 'Okay then.' I could hear the relief in his voice. 'I'll open the blinds.'

***

We relaxed on the island for the next few days and made the most of the villa and its beautiful surroundings. There were no further uninvited interruptions, but that didn't stop Richie constantly looked over his shoulder, forever guarded. The end of our holiday came too quickly, and I braced myself for what was about to happen when we touched down at home.

The helicopter ride was uneventful. At the mainland airport, however, Richie was keen to take me through duty-free. Obligingly, I followed him to the sunglasses stand, which displayed row upon row of stunning frames in all different shapes and sizes.

'Choose a pair.' Richie insisted.

Oh, I couldn't–'

'I want to buy you a present. If you don't choose, I'll have to choose for you.'

I stopped protesting. 'The bigger the better.' Richie winked.

After trying on what felt like a hundred pairs, I finally settled on some cat eye Prada sunglasses that covered most of my face. I looked at the price tag and almost choked, but Richie took them from me and paid for them at the till.

He slid them onto the bridge of my nose. 'Richie, you shouldn't have. They're beautiful,' I gushed, checking out my reflection in a mirror.

'Not half as beautiful as you,' he said softly. 'Anyway, you'll need them.'

As soon as we were back on English soil, Riche's phone began to ring. It was Aaron, his agent. 'Rich, there's paparazzi everywhere. We've got no way of holding them back.'

Richie took a deep breath. 'We'll just have to get it over with.' His tone was distant, almost military-like.

'Okay, I'll be waiting outside the doors.' Aaron rung off.

Richie took my hand and marched us through the airport. He didn't need to say another word; he knew I'd heard everything.

He squeezed my hand. 'Ready?'

'Ready as I'll ever be.'

He pushed the door open. I heard voices cry out as I was dazzled by flashing lights that seemed to come from every angle. The collective noise of various camera shutters sounded like a hundred crocodile snapping their jaws. Richie ploughed ahead. He kept his head down and took long strides. I had to scurry alongside him to keep up.

'Is this your new girlfriend?'

'Richie, what about your children?'

'Does your ex-wife know you've moved on so quickly?'

The crowd surged closer. I felt hot, nauseous, claustrophobic. Hands, from every direction, reached for me, grabbing anything they could. There was an onslaught of questions, each one with more intensity, more pressure. A camera was literally shoved in my face, and I had to shield my eyes from the incoming flash.

I let go of Richie. That was my biggest mistake.

I was swept away by the throng of hyenas. I glimpsed the horror on Richie's face as the mob swarmed.

'What's your name, pretty lady?'

'It's Penny, isn't it?'

'Did Richie buy you those glasses?'

Fingers clawed at me, and I thrashed out in blind panic. There was no escape. I felt like I was about to pass out when a hand reached into the centre of the frenzy. It was Richie plucking me from their clutches.

We bulldozed through the mass with even more vigour than before. Richie's lips were tight, his eyes, a fierce shade of blue. He focused on the airport doors with a steely determination.

We eventually made it outside and into Aaron's car, though flashes of light still burned in every direction. Cameras were pressed against the windows, fists banged on the car roof. *This must be how animals feel in a cage.*

Aaron set off but multiple cars pulled out in front of him. He swerved violently from left to right, trying to avoid being blocked in. Soon enough, he'd outmanoeuvred the paparazzi and the commotion ceased as we sped out of the airport car park. I stared out of the window, watching the world pass by in a blur. Richie lit a cigarette, and the smell of smoke engulfed the car.

'It's okay, Penny. They've gone now. We'll be safe when we're at the flat, you won't have to go through that again. Well, not today, at least.'

Flat? What flat?

It took me a few seconds to come to my senses. Tears rolled down my cheeks. I was hot and sweaty and felt like I could be sick at any moment. My voice trembled. 'I'd like to go home, please, Richie.'

'You'll be safe there, I promise. It's the best way of protecting you right now.' He tossed his cigarette butt out of the car window. 'There's electronic gates, fobs, CCTV, the lot. There's security in the lobby, 24/7. I've been living there since my divorce, and I've never had a problem. It's a haven, I promise you.'

'I want to go home, Richie,' I repeated, sternly. His face fell. After a moment he caught Aaron's eye in the rear-view mirror and gave him a nod.

Chapter Twenty-Four

'I will not have my daughter made to be a laughing-stock like this.' Dad threw down a pile of newspapers and gossip magazines, his face red and blotchy. No one responded. We'd already said everything that could be said.

It had been three days since Richie and I came home and the pictures of us at the airport were still circulating. Headlines were variations of the same thing: *Richie Falls For Poor Girl Penny; Age Doesn't Matter When You're Richie Clarke; Richie Clark: Sugar Daddy; From Rags to Richie.* They couldn't quite decide if I was too young or too poor for Richie.

'Maybe you should go see him.' Mum knew I was not normally this quiet. 'He's probably the best person for advice right now.'

Richie had tried to call me every day since we'd parted, but I hadn't answered. We'd exchanged a few words via text, enough for me to gather how worried he was about me. *Wouldn't seeing him make things worse?*

'I'll text him,' I mumbled. I left the room and the frown on Mum's face.

I got halfway up the stairs and heard Dad say in a low voice, 'He's not much of a man if he's leaving her to fend for herself.'

'He's tried, Darren. Penny's ignoring him,' Mum replied. 'He's stationed security around the house at least—didn't you see them on your way in? The only thing he hasn't done is come round himself. But that may be a wise move, given the circumstances. Especially if there's no guarantee Penny would even let him in.'

I closed my bedroom door and flopped onto the bed. What a mess. I just wanted it all to blow over so Richie

From Rags to Richie

and I could carry on where we left off. Now I was afraid to even leave the house. I missed Richie. Even though it had only been three days since I'd last seen him, it felt like a lifetime. So much had changed. Maybe Mum was right, he was the best person to speak to. I picked up my phone.

I want to see you.

His response was instant: *I'm on my way.*

Huh? Didn't he have important actor business to attend to? And it was only four o'clock in the afternoon—he wouldn't be able to come inside without being noticed. I typed back with trembling fingers. *Wait! What about the paparazzi?*

Fuck them. You're more important.

Richie was so sexy when he was angry, even via text.

Forty-five minutes later, a white Audi pulled up outside. My phone vibrated. It's me. Get in.

Tentatively, I opened our front door and looked around. There was no one in sight, but that didn't mean anything. The Audi flashed its lights and I scurried down the path, my Prada sunglasses tight on my face. When I opened the passenger door, my fears melted away. Richie looked positively delicious in jeans and a plain white T-shirt. He wore a huge pair of sunglasses, despite the Audi's tinted windows.

'New wheels?' I said.

'It's a hire car. The Benz is a little obvious.' He smiled and I noticed a smattering of stubble around his jawline. 'We can go back to my place, it's safe there.' He gave my thigh a reassuring squeeze.

We drove to his apartment block. The gates slowly swung open then closed behind us, like something out of a Batman movie.

Richie and I clearly had different definitions of a flat. What he actually lived in was a penthouse apartment, though I don't know why I expected anything less. It was the ultimate man cave, matte black and minimal, with every mod con you could think of. He gestured for me to sit on the sofa while he went into the kitchen and got us both a drink.

Richie's phone pinged on the coffee table. It was a message from someone called Hannah. *So, go on, who's the new arm candy?* it said. He returned from the kitchen and handed me a glass of wine. 'How are you doing?'

I was glad to have something that would help calm my nerves, and I felt a lot safer inside his apartment. 'I've been better,' I mumbled.

'I understand.' He sighed. 'It's not usually that bad. Grabbing you like that, it's not on. Aaron's looking into–'

I raised my hand. 'I'd rather not go into it all again if that's okay.'

We sat in silence. Richie sipped his drink and I fiddled with the stem of my wine glass.

'Carl called me today,' he said. 'The premiere of *Love and War* will be held in Leicester Square a few months from now.'

My eyes widened. Wow. But my face fell as I realised something. 'I won't get an invite though, will I?'

'Of course you will—you'll be my plus one. I wouldn't let you miss it for the world. That's if you want to go.'

I thought about it. Following the recent hype around our relationship, both of us being there would probably draw even more publicity. Could I handle that again? At least at the premiere, the press would be more professional. There would be barriers and security all around us. Sat beside Richie again, in the comfort of his four walls, I felt more confident than I had done over the last three days.

'Let me dress you.' The words fell out of my mouth.

He raised an eyebrow. 'So, does that mean you'll come?'

'I know you'll have the likes of Armani and Versace knocking on your door, but it would mean the world to me. You've done so many lovely things for me, and I've been searching for something I could do for you. This is my version of the Prada sunglasses.' Richie didn't appear convinced. 'How about you think about it, and I'll mock-up some designs?'

'Okay,' he said, bemused. I think he was just happy to see me smiling again.

We spent the rest of the afternoon chatting idly and covering each other in kisses until I felt it was time for me to leave.

'You don't want to talk about...' he trailed off.

Admittedly, asking his advice was the reason I'd got in touch. But now I was having a good time and I felt that bringing it up again would ruin the mood. I was excited about the premiere, where I'd have face the vultures again—maybe I'd get used to it eventually.

'No, thank you. Though I wouldn't mind a lift home in your fancy hire car.'

Chapter Twenty-Five

'I'm not sure how I feel about crushed velvet.'

I'd returned to Richie's apartment a week later with some sketches. It had been a blissful week, with nothing out of the ordinary occurring. The fascination with Richie and I showed signs of blowing over; I hadn't caught a glimpse of us in the press for nearly five days. I didn't leave the house without my sunglasses, though.

Richie carefully studied my design sketch.

'It's a bit out there, but trust me, you can pull this off.' I was desperate for him to like it.

'It's not a little 'in your face'?' He cocked his head to the side and closed one eye.

'You're the star of the production, Richie, you need to stand out! How about we do some window shopping? I've seen similar things on the high street...you can see what you think before I start work on this bespoke Penny J design. We can then get a bite to eat.'

'Okay. I'd like that.'

***

Lampposts were adorned with twinkling lights and shop windows brimmed with festive décor. It was late November and Christmas was creeping closer.

'Where to first?'

'Follow me.' I grabbed his hand and led him to Carnell's department store.

Party season was in full swing, and each store packed with glitz and glamour. In the menswear section, I found a few suits with a similar cut and colour of my design. Richie played along and tried several outfits. He looked incredibly handsome in every single one of them.

By the time we reached the fifth department store, Richie's stomach grumbled loudly.

'Okay, you win. You can make my suit.' He held his

From Rags to Richie

hands up in defeat. 'But only if we can get some food.'

'Are you serious?' I asked. 'Even the crushed velvet one?'

'Anything, if it means we can eat!'

'Okay, fine. But I'm ordering the fabric right now.' I loaded the website on my phone. 'There's no going back then.'

Richie didn't seem to mind. He wrapped his arm around my shoulders and guided me out of the shop. I had my head down, focused on my phone and the fabric wholesaler. Richie was concerned only with his ravenous stomach. Neither of us had a clue about what was waiting outside.

A throng of photographers appeared out of nowhere, their cameras ready for action. We walked right into them.

'Penny! Have you always gone for older men?'

'What's it like dating someone old enough to be your dad?'

Oh my god, the noise!

Richie tightened his grip and manoeuvred me through the mayhem.

'Were you his mistress when he was married?'

'Penny! How does it feel to be a home wrecker?'

I had a sudden realisation. They were out for me, not Richie. My breath hitched in my throat and my heart pounded in my chest as numerous arms reached for me and cameras were shoved in my face. There was a thunderstorm of shutters opening and closing, rivalled only by the booming voices of the reporters.

'Penny! Does he spoil you?'

'Penny! Are you the reason Richie's getting divorced?'

'Penny! Penny! Penny!'

Richie barged through them and got us to the pavement edge where he hailed a passing taxi. Once we were inside, he yelled at the driver to move. I clung to Richie on the back seat; he rubbed my back soothingly. Though we managed to pull away quickly, the damage had been done. Tears streamed from my eyes and dampened Richie's jacket.

'Food?' Richie whispered. I shook my head—my appetite had completely vanished. 'Okay, a film and a takeaway it is. But text your mum, you're staying with me tonight.'

I lifted my head to protest, but he shook his head. 'I'm not taking no for an answer this time. I can't have you disappearing on me again.' He kissed my forehead and I obediently reached for my phone.

Chapter Twenty-Six

Hours later, unable to sleep, I watched the sunrise. I left Richie snoozing in its golden glow and flopped onto the sofa, scrolling through my phone. My face appeared over and over again beneath tacky headlines that screamed accusations, which had clearly provoked the keyboard warriors. Strangers. People who didn't even know me, making my life their business. I clicked on each photograph, zoomed in, picked them apart. I knew paparazzi shots were rarely glamorous, but I didn't look happy in any of them, and neither did Richie. A week ago, I'd convinced myself that I could handle this. Right now, I wasn't so sure.

Last night had been lovely. Richie treated me like a princess and catered to my every whim, trying his best to help me forget about it all. But I knew I couldn't live like this. Neither of us could. That perfect day, destroyed by one moment. What Richie and I had was special, but I couldn't live indoors for the rest of my life or forever look over my shoulder—no matter how perfect the man might be. It was equally unfair to put Richie through this whenever the paparazzi was on the prowl; it was exhausting.

I sat down at the kitchen island with a piece of paper and pen. I wanted to write Richie a letter, explaining how I felt, but I couldn't find the words. I stared angrily at the blank page. *Focus, Penny. Just write what comes into your head...!*

I'm just a poor boy, I need no sympathy.
Because I'm easy come, easy go, little high, little low.
Any way the wind blows doesn't really matter to me.

Queen's words poured out of me and made tears well in my eyes. This really was it. We'd had our little high, our little low, and now it was time for me to go.

I'm sorry, Richie. Our worlds are just too different. I hope you understand.

I heard movement in the bedroom. I grabbed the note and stuffed it into my handbag, then wiped away my tears with the sleeve of my sweatshirt. Richie came into the kitchen, wearing only black boxers.

'I've just realised...don't you need to measure me?' he said mischievously.

I spent a good hour with my measuring tape in hand, taking Richie's proportions for a suit I was probably never going to make. I still enjoyed the opportunity to splay my hands across his skin. What started as a practical task soon turned into fun and games, as things often did with Richie. Before long, he'd scooped me up, tossed aside the tape measure and carried me to the bedroom.

***

A few hours later we were on Richie's sofa watching nonsense on TV. His phone rang and I saw Aaron's name on his screen.

'Mind if I take this?'

'Go ahead.'

He went into the bedroom to answer it and closed the door behind him. A wave of nausea hit me. *He's beautiful but this is tragic. One minute I'm in paradise, the next, I'm on the precipice of Hell.*

We had to end things...I genuinely couldn't see another way. I retrieved the note from my bag and placed it on the kitchen counter, along with the Prada sunglasses. They were such a thoughtful, kind gift, but they were a reminder of bad times. With a deep sigh, I took one last look around Richie's apartment. I left before I changed my mind.

Once outside, I put my earphones in and pressed play on my phone. Right on cue, Freddie Mercury took the spotlight.

'Goodbye, everybody, I've got to go.

Got to leave you all behind and face the truth.'

When I got home, Mum was in the kitchen. As soon as I saw her, I burst into tears. She hugged me for the longest time. 'What's happened?' she whispered.

'I've ended it.' I whispered back.

Chapter Twenty-Seven

Richie called me around ten times a day and texted constantly. His emotions ranged from surprise to anger to sadness. I didn't respond. I didn't feel strong enough to face him, so I just didn't. He'd appeared in my life quite suddenly—why was it so difficult for him to disappear?

One afternoon, I was home alone, and the doorbell rang. I was too nervous to answer it—scared that it was Richie, or worse, a reporter wanting a story. A slip of paper was pushed through the letterbox; once I was sure the person posting it had gone, I learned there was a package waiting for me in the wheelie bin. I crept out of the front door like a mischievous child, retrieved the parcel and raced up to my room. I ripped open the packaging and felt the luxurious softness of crushed velvet. It was the material for Richie's suit. I groaned as yet more tears threatened to spill over my cheeks.

Then a thought struck me. Instead of wallowing in my bed all day, why not channel all my energy into something more useful than self-pity? Why not give Richie something to remember me by and the paparazzi something else to write about?

***

I spent the next couple of weeks locked away in my bedroom, practically chained to my sewing machine.

Richie still called every day; he even visited once. I heard his smooth voice from the top of the stairs as he stood on the doorstep and pleaded with Mum to see me. As much as I yearned for him, I couldn't see him again, it would be too much to bear. Mum sent him on his way quietly and I heard the sadness in his voice. It broke my heart, but it gave me even more motivation to get back to my sewing.

I had other visitors, too—Mum, Dad and Aunt Ange came to talk to me while I worked. I barely left my room until the suit was complete, just to eat and take the occasional shower.

A week before the premiere, I ventured outdoors, to the post office. I'd poured my heart into that garment. I sent it to Riche's address via next day delivery.

***

The day after the premiere was my first shift back behind the counter at Belle's Boutique. Aunt Ange had offered me my old job as soon as she heard of the breakup; she also said to take as long as I needed, until I felt ready to show my face in public again.

I woke that day and found no headlines blackening my name. It appeared I was free. I was finally old news.

At Belle's Boutique, I was struck by how little had changed, given how much had happened since I'd last been there. Ultimately, I knew that it was me who had changed. In the time I'd been away from the shop, I'd experienced so much of what the world had to offer— the good and the bad. Now, I was more than happy to back in the place I'd once likened to a ball and chain. *I'll never take this place for granted again.*

Aunt Ange returned from her morning coffee run with two cappuccinos and a newspaper, a small smile on her lips. 'You need to see this,' she said, plonking the paper in front of me. She opened it at the celebrity gossip pages.

I groaned, fearing the worst. 'Aunt Ange, come on. Can we not?'

She didn't take any notice of me. 'Just because you don't work for them anymore, or date Richie Clarke anymore, doesn't mean we can't celebrate your achievements. You were as much a part of that production as the rest of them. And you won't be disappointed with the coverage, trust me.'

I sighed in defeat. My passion project had worked; creating Richie's suit had helped to heal my wounds.

I wasn't ready to see his face, but Aunt Ange was insistent.

When I finally turned my attention to the paper, my jaw hit the floor. Centre stage was a full-length photo of Richie in my suit. I couldn't believe it. I stared at the page, open-mouthed, for what felt like an eternity. He'd worn it, just like he promised.

I looked up at Aunt Ange, whose face was glowing with pride. 'Read the caption, honey.'

I scanned the text below Richie's photo: *Man of the hour, alone on the red carpet, Richie Clarke wears a suave crushed velvet number in royal blue. Made by up-and-coming designer PJ Mercury, Clarke informed us. Not the obvious choice, but isn't that what the ladies love about him? And your luck is in, girls—Richie breezed along the carpet, free, single, and ready to mingle.*

Aunt Ange scooped me into a hug when she realised I was crying. Hot, wet tears streamed down my face, and I leaned into her embrace without saying a word.

PJ Mercury. Richie had done exactly what I did, when what he wanted to say was too hard; he let *Queen* take the lead.

Leaning my head on her shoulder, Aunt Ange and I read through the rest of the article. *Love and War* looked like it was going to be a huge success. Even Win got her five minutes of fame, with a tiny photo in the corner of her and Craig, arm in arm.

The chime of the doorbell indicated that we had our first customer of the day. We were greeted by a disgruntled Mrs Delong.

'Go freshen up, love,' Aunt Ange whispered. 'I've got this.'

Gratefully, I headed to the staff room, the image of Richie in my crushed velvet creation still on my mind. Despite my tears, I hadn't felt joy like this in weeks— even Mrs Delong's complaints couldn't take that away from me.

Chapter Twenty-Eight

'Maybe someday we will find that it wasn't really wasted time.' ~ The Eagles

Richie didn't expect the door handle to feel so familiar in the palm of his hand, but it did. It still felt like home. The smell of cinnamon and orange wafted through the air as he entered the house.

'Dad!' Timmy came running first, his blonde curls bouncing. 'Daddy!' His younger brother followed straight after, as per usual.

'Hey, scamps!' Richie knelt down, scooping them both in his arms and squeezing them so tightly he thought they may squeal. Their embrace was filled with such warmth and love; Richie never wanted to let them go again.

'Are you staying?' said Hannah. Everything about her was elegant—from her long blonde hair, fastened back by a tortoiseshell clip, to the silk dress that draped from her waist. Richie shot her a quizzical look.

'You're still wearing your coat, Richard,' she added. For once, since this whole mess began, she wasn't being vicious.

Richie let go of the boys and unzipped his coat. Hannah tugged it off his shoulders and hung it on the coat stand. 'Make yourself at home.' She gestured to the living room. 'Drink?'

'Yes please.' The couple had agreed to be civil in front of their boys, but this was entirely out of character.

'Coffee? Something stronger?' Hannah lingered in the doorway as the boys snuggled next to their father on the sofa.

'Coffee would be great, thanks.' Richie's voice was hoarse, his throat suddenly dry.

'No problem.' She sauntered into the kitchen,

and Richie took a moment to revel in the familiar surroundings. Everything was just how he'd left it almost a year ago. The only difference was a new, larger than life Christmas tree that took pride of place in the bay window. Its baubles glistened in the setting sun. He was overcome by feelings of nostalgia. I miss this house, my home.

He noticed George leaning precariously over the edge of the sofa, trying to reach something. 'Everything okay, champ?' Richie moved to help him.

'I'm trying to find my book. Daddy's fave.'

'You can read it to us,' said Timmy, fiddling with the bottom of his T-shirt. 'Like you used to.'

Richie's heart broke.

***

On Christmas morning, Richie woke to the sound of tiny feet padding along the landing and whispers outside the door of the guest bedroom. 'Wake Daddy and go downstairs!' George said excitedly.

'No, don't,' warned Timmy.

There was a long pause; for a moment he thought they'd gone back to their bedrooms. Then he heard George's voice again. 'Pleeease, Timmy! I wanna see if Santa's been!'

Timmy was solemn. 'What if Daddy gets mad and leaves again?'

They both fell silent. Richie had to swallow hard to fight the lump in his throat. He was about to get up when he heard Hannah's voice. 'Boys, back to bed! Do you know what time it is? Your father needs his rest, he's a busy man. Have you both opened your stockings already?'

After a mumbled response, he heard the boys slink back to their rooms. A few minutes later there was a soft knock on the door and Hannah entered, a tray of warm toast and tea in her hand.

'Hey,' she said softly. 'Breakfast?' She looked maidenly in her long, white, silk dressing gown. She was the traditional English rose. She perched on the edge of the bed and handed Richie the tray. Amongst the tea and toast was a small wooden box.

'Merry Christmas,' she whispered.

He lifted the lid of the box. Deep down, he knew what was in there and it made his stomach do somersaults. Resting on the cushion was a single gold band—his wedding ring. The ring he'd returned to her just twelve months ago. He stared at it, unable to think of a single word to say.

'I've been thinking a lot about us, and I want to make things right. Start again from where we left off,' she suggested.

'Hannah, I can't. I'm sorry.' He snapped the ring box closed.

'It's not because of that girl, is it?' Fire flashed in her eyes. Richie didn't answer and stared intently at the breakfast tray instead.

'I don't want to fight.' She reached for his hand and squeezed it gently. 'Just say you'll think about it, Richard. For the kids, but most of all, for me.' She watched him earnestly. 'I've made up my mind. This whole situation between us is stupid. I've no idea how we ended up like this, but it's time to fix it.'

A long pause stretched out between them.

'I don't know what to say.' Richie finally met her gaze.

She sighed. 'I don't want you to say anything, not right now. Just think about it. Take your time.' She stood up. 'I know that, eventually, you'll see that I'm right. It just makes sense. You've had your fun, now it's time to come home.'

The rest of Christmas Day passed in a warm blur. They played 'happy families' for the sake of the kids as the wooden box and the proposal it held burned a hole in Richie's pocket.

***

A week later, Richie pulled up outside Penny's house, with its quaint box hedge and leaded windows. Tears sprung. Everything Richie had bottled up exploded as he succumbed to his emotions.

He didn't see Penny leave her house. He didn't see her face appear at the car window, shocked and confused. But he felt her. She put her arms around him and coaxed him out of the driver's seat.

'I need you to know that the feelings I had for you were real.' The words came tumbling out. 'You weren't just another notch on my bedpost, Penelope James. At one point, you were the only reason I was breathing.'

They were in the middle of the street, exposed to the world. Vulnerable and unguarded. Surprisingly, she didn't seem to notice. All she cared about in that moment was him. And he her. Nothing else seemed to matter.

'You've always been the one I wanted. I was planning a way to win you back and then...' Richie realised he'd pulled the ring box from his coat pocket without even meaning to. The box felt heavy in his hand, like it was weighing down his whole arm, dragging him down. Without saying a word, Penny took the little box and lifted the lid. He watched the realisation of what lay inside wash over her. Tears welled in her eyes.

'I think you already know what you need to do, Richie.' Her voice trembled.

She wrapped her arms around him again and he heard the click of the box's lid closing. As they drew apart, he felt her hesitate. She looked at his face intently, as if committing it to memory—taking in every detail, every line, every freckle, every flaw. She closed the gap between them, and he kissed her like she was the only person in the world. Their lips pressed together so hard it almost hurt. Then she pulled away.

'Goodbye, Richie,' she whispered. She pushed something into one of his palms and placed the wooden box in the other.

'We can keep in touch though, right? Stay friends? I can still wear PJ Mercury to all my events, can't I?'

Richie knew he sounded desperate, but he didn't care. She tried to smile, but the tears rolled steadily down her cheeks. 'This doesn't have to be the end, does it? We can be together, just in a different way.'

Penny shook her head and looked down. She kept opening her mouth as if to speak, but then she'd close it again. She looked so broken.

She met his gaze. 'We both know that's not a good idea. This is goodbye, Richie. Our worlds are just too different.'

'You're right,' He heard his own voice break. They stood in silence for a moment, just holding hands in the middle of the street.

'I've got to go now,' she said quietly.

He felt those three unspoken words. They hung in the air. 'I'll never forget you, Penny James.'

She smiled. That was the image of her he wanted to keep. The moment he always wanted to remember.

She went back inside and Richie got back in his car. Her front door closed behind her and that was it, he was out of her life. For good.

He took a moment to gather his thoughts. One door had closed, and another one had opened. A new chapter. A clean slate. An old new. Everything had changed, yet nothing was different.

He opened the palm of his left hand and found his wedding ring. Penny had taken it out of the box and placed it in his other hand, ensuring it was ready and waiting for him. Her unspoken blessing. He slid it back on his finger and started the car.

THE END

Acknowledgements

I want to thank my nearest and dearest for their ongoing support...you spur me on to do what I was made to do.

Thank you to my husband, for being my biggest cheerleader. I definitely wouldn't have two books under my belt without you.

To my parents and the puppy—thanks for putting up with me abandoning you for my 'pop up office' time.

Thank you to my publisher, editor, writing guru and everything in-between, for continuing to turn my dreams into reality.

Thank you, NaNoWriMo, for motivating me to get this story on paper in the first place.

And, finally, huge, huge thanks to my lovely readers. Hearing your wonderful feedback makes my heart sing and keeps me writing!